The
FIRE CATS
of
LONDON

Also by Anna Fargher

The Umbrella Mouse
Umbrella Mouse to the Rescue

The
FIRE CATS
of
LONDON

ANNA FARGHER

ILLUSTRATED BY SAM USHER

MACMILLAN CHILDREN'S BOOKS

First published 2022 by Macmillan Children's Books
an imprint of Pan Macmillan
The Smithson, 6 Briset Street, London EC1M 5NR
EU representative: Macmillan Publishers Ireland Ltd, 1st Floor,
The Liffey Trust Centre, 117–126 Sheriff Street Upper
Dublin 1, D01 YC43
Associated companies throughout the world
www.panmacmillan.com

ISBN 978-1-5290-4687-8

Text copyright © Anna Fargher 2022
Illustrations copyright © Sam Usher 2022

1 3 5 7 9 8 6 4 2

A CIP catalogue record for this book is available from the British Library.

Printed and bound by CPI Group (UK) Ltd, Croydon CR0 4YY

For Eliza

CHAPTER ONE

THE WILDCATS

In the hours before dawn, two young wildcats stalked through the scrubland behind their mother, padding stealthily along the edges of the pine forest, swaying gently in a cool summer breeze. No rain had fallen for weeks, and the ground was crisp under their paws. The young wildcats had already grown out of their soft kitten fur and they were getting stronger and bolder every day. Each nightly outing with their mother was a new adventure, and they mirrored her steps, parting the long grass with their striated heads as they scanned the ground for prey with their large eyes, glowing in the light of the sinking moon.

The wildcats halted, their ears pricking towards a small, unsuspecting rabbit. Rigid with anticipation, Asta held her breath beside her brother and silently willed him not to make a sound. They watched their mother slowly edge forward and stop now and again with an upraised paw to scent the air and the prey, nibbling the grass ahead.

Their mother's ears flattened as she crouched low and froze. Then, in a flash, she pounced on the rabbit and somersaulted twice across the ground. Asta's and Ash's pulses raced as a brief scuffle ensued before the wind sighed through the trees and everything was still once more.

She turned to her young and nodded softly, inviting them to approach.

Asta pounced on Ash and knocked him on to his side. 'Come on!' she cried, leaving him to wriggle upright in the grass.

'Wait, Asta,' Ash panted as Asta bounded ahead through the scrub. 'Not so fast!'

But Asta didn't hear him. She reached her mother and met her head rub with a purr. Asta marvelled at how easy the hunt had been. The rabbit had never seen their mother coming, and its death had been as quick and merciful as it should have been.

Asta and Ash had not mastered being predators yet. So far, all the prey they'd neared had escaped unharmed.

'How do you do it, Mother?' Ash mewed, catching up with Asta and joining their mother beside her third kill of the night.

Ash looked up at her longingly, but instead of a head rub

she gave him a knowing glance. 'You'll both learn once you quiet the hunger to be the first to succeed.'

Asta and Ash met each other's gazes with flicking tails. They hated being told what to do, and competing against each other was a thrill neither of them wanted to cease. To be the first to make a kill would prove they were strong and ready to venture into the world alone. Ash hung his head each time Asta gained ground. She was too swift and bold, and a playful cuff behind the ear sometimes led to a scrap.

'Look!' Ash gasped, his sharp eyes catching a shooting star blazing across the sky above. 'I've never seen one with a long tail like that!'

'That's because it's rare,' their mother replied, craning her head upwards with Asta and watching it streak across the night. 'Shooting stars signal change. Perhaps it's a sign you will soon be ready to fend for yourselves.'

Asta and Ash stared at one another, their hackles rising with mischievousness. A second later, they attacked and gently bit and clawed at one another's fur as they rolled across the ground.

Their mother sighed and a soft smile drew across her tabby face, for she didn't mind her young staying by her side a little longer.

'Don't grow up *too* fast, my loves.'

*

Sunrise was scorching the sky red when the wildcats finally travelled back to their den. It was deep inside the hollow of a tree that had fallen in the outskirts of the forest long ago. Asta had begged for them to stay out and practise, long after Ash and their mother had wanted to return home, but their hunting was no better. Asta and Ash had frightened away every mouse, vole and rabbit they'd encountered, yet by the time the birds began singing their first

morning melodies their mother had made sure that their bellies were full, their spirits were high and their enthusiasm for the next hunt remained strong.

Nearing their den, the three wildcats crossed the treeline with the leaves flurrying overhead and their mother slowed to smell the wind. Asta and Ash did the same, catching a strange scent floating on the air. They cocked their ears. Their mother's pupils dilated. She scanned the thicket and Asta's senses pricked, a cold feeling of dread crawling over her fur.

A twig snapped. 'Run!' their mother cried. 'Hurry! Get back to our tree!'

A tall shrub to the left burst to life. Two men – one long and lean, the other short and stout – emerged from the brush with two hounds that whimpered with excitement as they watched the cats bolt into the woods.

Asta didn't dare look back. With her blood pounding through her limbs, she sprinted towards a bed of thick ground ferns growing in the depths of the forest, praying it would conceal them. She couldn't see Ash or her mother, but from the sound of rustling of leaves and shallow breaths behind her she sensed they were at her heels.

They raced on with the thudding of the men's boots echoing in their ears. The men's shouts were rapidly growing louder, and Asta knew by their urgent and impatient tone that the wildcats must be getting away. Seeing the bracken ahead, she picked up speed. She willed for Ash and her mother to do the same and she felt a rush of relief as she realized that the crunch of the men's footsteps had abruptly disappeared.

BANG!

The tremendous noise made every bird perched in the trees above take flight in a cacophony of squawks and clattering wings.

The wildcats scattered through the undergrowth in panic. Asta swerved sharply to the right and leaped to the nearest tree. She scrambled up its rugged bark to a high bough and crept forward along the branch, hidden in the treetops by a screen of green leaves. Trembling, she searched for Ash and her mother below, and stared helplessly as they scrambled separately towards the bracken, each with a man and his hound pursuing them.

The men stopped, their dogs obediently heeling beside them, their tails wagging. Their masters lifted long muskets to their shoulders.

'RUN!' Asta yelled, but Ash and their mother were too far away to hear her. She lost sight of her family fleeing through the trees, and her breath halted in her throat.

BANG!

Asta yelped, feeling the boom of the rifle thunder through her.

BANG!

BANG!

A sickening silence unfurled through the forest.

'Go on, boy!' a voice ordered, and the two hounds scampered through the undergrowth. The men followed, walking through a white mist trickling from their muskets.

Asta couldn't believe this was happening. Only a moment ago, her family was getting ready to curl up in their den and nestle into each other's fur.

Asta scanned the forest for the two men. She smouldered as she found them, far off in the distance, standing in the middle of the bed of bracken with their hounds wriggling triumphantly at their feet.

The stout man was bending low and patting the dogs. He stood tall and held something that crushed Asta's heart.

It was a wildcat.

CHAPTER TWO

THE DEN

Tears flooded Asta's eyes. She willed their mother to move – to fight, to run – but she dangled listlessly, as if she was asleep in the stout man's grasp.

The men and the hounds walked deeper into the woods. Asta trailed them, creeping along the length of the tree branch until it thinned and buckled under her weight. Wobbling there in the breeze, she looked fearfully about the group and searched for Ash in the taller man's grip, but the stout man, striding behind him, blocked her view.

Asta felt sick watching these monsters walk away after sneaking into her home. These men and their machines had no claws or teeth; they didn't honour the dead with a chance to defend themselves in a fight. They stole the lives of others from afar with weapons against which no animal stood a chance. Her hackles stiffened. She wanted to hurt them. To rip them open.

The men disappeared behind tall shrubs and Asta hurried back along the bough to the tree trunk and hurtled down it, scrabbling along the rough surface with much more difficulty than the climb. But the need to find Ash gave her courage, and she leaped and landed on the forest floor with a thump.

Keeping her ears and eyes pricked for danger, she bounded towards the thicket where the humans had turned. Slowing to stalk around it, and finding no sign of them or their dogs, she picked up pace again and scanned the forest for the men. The birds were chirruping loudly now that the sun had fully risen, and Asta resented them singing so joyously without caring that her mother and brother had been taken.

On and on she ran until she found herself in a part of the forest she had never seen before. Ahead, the thick woodland parted into a grassy corridor that stretched into the distance between the trees, casting shivering patterns of bright dappled sunlight on to the ground. Two horses grazed there, harnessed to a rustic wooden wagon. At the back of it, the two men were shuffling an array of tools and boxes while their hounds watched, sitting on their haunches and wagging their tails. Asta crept into some brambles and watched.

'The traps snared us a couple of badgers,' the stout man noted, 'four hedgehogs, a stoat and an otter.'

'And we shot six rabbits,' the tall man added, 'a fox, two beavers, four crows and this beauty of a wildcat.'

'How'd you know it ain't just some tabby?'

'It's bigger for a start,' the taller man replied with the authority of experience. 'And see its blunt, bushy tail? Tabbies ain't got them – they've got skinny tails without these thick black rings.'

'I've heard some parishes can give a whole shilling for a wildcat.'

'And we'll get even more when we sell the fur. They say nothin's warmer than a wildcat pelt.'

'I reckon them apothecaries in London will give us a fine sum for all its other parts as well. A wildcat potion cured my headaches once.'

London. Asta recognized the name. Their mother had mentioned it.

'Same goes for the rest of today's catch if we can deliver them before they spoil.' The tall man gleefully slapped the stouter man on the back. 'The apothecaries will be clawing for this booty. We've got enough here to stuff their shelves

11

with medicine for months. Let's get movin'. We need to collect the bounty from the churchwarden before we journey back to London along the Devil's Highway. If we hurry and aren't bothered by any of them land pirates, we'll reach the city this evening.'

The men put the dead animals inside the boxes and covered their haul with canvas that they stretched over the wagon and hooked tightly to its wooden frame.

Hate swept through Asta. She was a fast sprinter. If she rushed at these men, she could rake them with her claws and make them pay for hurting her and her family, then she could escape into the treetops just like she'd done before. But, as she edged out of the brambles, she stopped. The humans had only mentioned *one* wildcat. That meant Ash must be alive, perhaps injured somewhere.

She glowered at the humans, longing for justice, but a moment later her throat tightened. She couldn't avenge her mother as she wanted. If her plan went wrong, and the men or the dogs killed her, then Ash would be alone. They needed each other now more than ever.

With tears misting her sight, she was slowly creeping out of the brambles when her rear left paw snagged on a knot of thorns. Gasping in pain, she shook herself free. The hounds snapped their heads towards her at once, ears pricked.

Every muscle in Asta's body tensed. The dogs jumped to their paws, their eyes alert and blazing as they trotted to the undergrowth where Asta was hiding.

The stout man whistled in a shrill pitch that seared Asta's ears.

'Come here, boys!' he called, patting the footboard at the front of the cart. The hounds halted, staring in Asta's direction. She held her breath and forced herself to ignore every instinct screaming for her to run away.

The tall man clapped his hands hard, twice. 'OI!' he boomed, and the hounds instantly turned their heads towards their master. 'Get inside, you little blighters!'

Asta felt a surge of relief. The dogs obediently trotted to the front of the wagon and launched themselves onto its front footboard. The thin man lifted a hinged plank of wood at the back of the cart and bolted it shut while the stout man clambered to the seating platform and yanked the horses' heads from the grass with long, leather reins. There was a cold crack of a whip and the cart moved into the grassy corridor between the trees.

Asta charged from the brambles, away from the cart. With a glance over her shoulder, she uttered a last choked goodbye to her mother. Her body ached with grief, knowing she would never see the glint of affection in her mother's green eyes, hear her purr before she fell asleep or feel the brush of her fur against hers again. She didn't know what to do without her mother. She'd always been there to listen to her troubles and to help her make sense of the world. Her one hope was finding Ash, but she swallowed, a terrible thought creeping into her mind. What if she had lost him too?

Asta hurried towards their den, but no matter how fast she ran she felt as if she was struggling through mud, and, although the forest was the same as it had always been, everything was different. Each time the trees creaked, a chill crawled up her spine, and as the leaves rustled in the early morning breeze Asta's ears flattened, catching sinister sounds on the wind.

She was panting from the sprint when she finally arrived at the hollow tree trunk. She paused beside it, cocking her ears, her green eyes scanning the undergrowth for danger before she slunk inside. She breathed deeply, feeling comforted by the familiar earthy smell of home.

'Ash?' she mewed, but all she heard was birdsong and the sound of a woodpecker drumming against the distant trees.

Her heart began to thud.

The den was empty.

Asta curled up in the same place in which she'd woken up with her mother and brother every day since she was born and wept, not knowing what to do. Their smell lingered where she lay and, as she closed her eyes, she could almost hear their steady, sleeping breaths.

For the rest of the morning, she willed Ash to return, but not even a fly or a spider neared the den. She was too scared to abandon it to search for him. It was the only place she felt safe, and every time she considered leaving it the image of the men and the dogs suddenly bursting from the thicket plagued her with fear. The forest was dense. There were hundreds of trees and shrubs for more monsters to hide behind, and if she dared to roam the woods they could strike at any time.

But, as the hours wore on, the thought of Ash hurt somewhere, hiding, snagged at her. She was sure he would try to find her if he could. If he was injured somewhere, he'd be scared, alone and in pain.

Asta drew a deep, shaky breath. She inched forward and peered from the hollow tree. The forest unfurled in every direction. Ash could be anywhere. The woodland was huge and her mother had only ever shown them the outskirts. Wildcats didn't need to venture far because they hunted along its borders where their prey fed on the grass and heather.

She tried to imagine what Ash would have done when the hunters came. He'd have been just as terrified as she'd been. He must have sheltered somewhere out of sight, like she had, but there were countless warrens, dens and treetops where he could have sought refuge. She sighed sadly as she remembered the days when they'd played hide-and-seek. He had won every time.

She stalked through the woods and flinched at every sudden gust of wind flurrying the leaves. She scoured the treetops and the bracken fronds, reluctant to blink in case she would miss a sign of him.

Bulging dark clouds were edging towards the bright afternoon sun when, in the distance ahead, she spied striped legs and a blunt, black, ringed tail lying flat and unmoving beneath the bracken that undulated in the summer breeze.

Asta's spirit leaped, and she bounded towards her brother, but, as she neared, the clouds shrouded the sun, plunging the forest into shadow. She had seen nothing but a cruel trick of the sunlight mottling the ground.

The rain pitter-pattered through the trees, and tears brimmed in Asta's eyes as the heavy raindrops thumped against her fur. She'd searched everywhere she knew Ash might be and, now that the rain had come, his scent would soon be washed away. She looked over her shoulder into the deep woods. She had sworn she would never enter without her mother, but it was her last hope.

Racing against the deluge, Asta bounded into the unfamiliar trees. She breathed deeply, trying to detect a hint of Ash on the air, but all she could smell was the fresh scent of a storm.

As the afternoon drew into evening, Asta's desperation made her bolder. She poked her head into warrens, whose rabbits squealed and kicked clouds of earth into her face.

She called for Ash inside a set,
but a badger rushed at her,
swiping its long, black claws.

A river, its surface hopping with raindrops, tempted her
further still and, worrying Ash had fallen in and been
dragged downstream, she followed
it to a large pile of
twigs and branches
stacked across the
water. She hurried,
stumbling on the
branches' slippery,
uneven surface,

and was swiftly berated not only by the beavers, but also an otter and her young.

The rain stopped and a mackerel sky blazed ochre and red when Asta padded back to the den wet, hungry and exhausted. This was all her fault. If she hadn't made them stay out and hunt, they might never have crossed paths with the men. She wished she'd never wanted to grow up so fast. She would do anything to go back and tell her mother and Ash how much they meant to her, and rub her head against theirs and press their noses together one last time.

CHAPTER THREE

ASH

For two days and nights, Asta combed the forest for Ash. At first, hunger gnawed at her, and she chewed grass, berries and bracken to quieten it. Even if she could have hunted alone, she had no urge to eat and, as the days passed, the hunger numbed, and she continued wandering restlessly through the places where her family had roamed.

On the third morning, there was still no sign of Ash, and the time without food and shelter took hold. Heavy with fatigue, she padded through a heath of bright yellow gorse bushes. She crumpled to the ground, feeling too weak with grief to care that she was exposed in the open air. The world was too hard and cruel, and to exist in it alone was too bleak and lonely for her to bear.

She was drifting into a heady, worn-out sleep when she heard it.

She blinked, not recognizing the sound. The fog of exhaustion and sadness clouded her senses, muffling it as though it was nothing but distant thunder.

A chattering of starlings was the first to fly overhead. The rooks, wood pigeons, blackbirds and woodpeckers were next, followed by the nightingales, jays and chaffinches, all squawking and screeching and clattering their wings in urgent flight.

It came again, louder this time. Horror scuttled over Asta's fur.

The humans and their dogs had returned.

She cursed herself for abandoning the den. If she raced into the forest now, she risked being seen or tracked by the hounds. Asta looked around the heath of gorse. At their highest, the bushes were not much taller than a man and the branches lacked the breadth of a sturdier tree. There would be little refuge if she climbed them. Her ears flattened, hearing the men guffaw and whistle for their dogs. She scrambled beneath a shrub and shuffled as far back into the thicket as she could.

Crouching low, she stared out over the heath. She could see clearly through the gaps between the thorny gorse stems and she swallowed, knowing that meant she could also be seen.

Panting neared, and Asta froze, smelling the stale scent of dogs' breath waft through the air. A flash of a dog's white fur, mottled with patches of brown, trotted alongside the gorse bush, closely followed by another hound. She bared her claws, dread thundering. A moment later, the dogs scampered on with their tails wagging high in the air, yet Asta's relief was short-lived as the stomp of footsteps thudded the ground. The two men came to a standstill beside her. She glared at their leather boots and hooked her claws into the earth.

The stout man paused to light a long clay pipe, and Asta recoiled, scenting tobacco for the first time.

'Put that out, you daft dandiprat!' the thin man scolded, snatching the pipe and tipping its contents on to the ground. He crushed its smouldering bulb with the toe of his boot. 'The animals will sniff ya a mile off. Ain't I taught you anything?'

'But we've been out here since before dawn and I ain't had a gasp today,' the stout man complained. 'I spent my takings on this new Virginian crop from Mad Rathder's Apothecary Shop. It'll dry out if it ain't smoked.'

The thin man clipped the back of the stout man's skull with his hand. 'The bigger our catch, the bigger your next pile of baccy will be, but you'll scare it all off with this muck, you pillock!' The stout man hung his head and Asta's blood pounded in her ears. If he turned, he would spot her, cowering in the gorse. 'And the day is still young,' the thin man went on. 'We've got more game to harvest before we set up camp for the night.'

Asta hummed with fresh worry for Ash.

Just then, a pheasant burst from the brush with a loud crow of alarm. The dogs charged after it and the men hurried forward, lifting their muskets to their shoulders.

The boom from the guns rattled every bone in Asta's body. She bolted from the gorse and tore through the heath without daring to look back.

Panic flooded Asta's senses. Her only thought was reaching the den where she knew she would be safe, and she hoped that if Ash was still alive he would head there too.

She was wheezing as she neared the bed of bracken where she had last seen her family alive. She tried to run faster but she stumbled, a delirious yellow mist fogging her sight as the days without sleep or food weakened her limbs. Dizzy with fear, she forced herself upright and staggered on.

It was then that her nose twitched, recognizing something that reminded her of Ash and her mother. She sniffed again, unsure if it was real. But there it was. An unmistakable smell she knew so well from their days together, and she swerved away from the path towards the den and dashed towards the scent.

It was growing stronger as she neared a thick shrub with a long, gloomy tunnel hidden within its lower leaves that was frequently used by the animals in the forest as a shortcut to the grasslands. Her heady desperation to be with Ash made her hurtle through it, and her heart heaved as she imagined seeing her brother's face again.

She had almost reached the other side when she spied a dead rabbit lying in the shadows. But, before she could slow, her paws met something cool and smooth under a scattering of loose earth.

A loud clang sounded behind her. Asta skidded and tumbled over the dead rabbit and her body smashed against a screen of grated metal. Yowling in confusion, she hurled herself against it, but it was stuck fast. She turned and rushed back the way she'd come, but the path back to the bracken was gone. A wall of cold wrought iron had taken its place.

Asta's stomach lurched.

She was trapped.

CHAPTER FOUR

THE HUNTERS

Asta's thoughts skittered for a way out. She bit and clawed and threw herself against the cage, hoping to break its hinges or damage its frame so she could squeeze through a gap and escape, but the heavy trap merely rattled where it was buried into the ground.

In the darkness of the leafy tunnel, she couldn't tell how much time had passed when she eventually surrendered to exhaustion. She collapsed beside the dead rabbit, detesting it for luring her to her doom.

The next morning, fear seized every muscle in Asta's body, hearing their footsteps approach. She shrank against the cage walls and silently begged them to walk on by, but the acrid smell of human sweat closed in. The dogs pushed their wet noses through the veil of leaves and pressed their nostrils against the trap. They sniffed vigorously, scenting her, and their yips and snuffles mounted.

Asta swatted her claws in a surge of spite. The dogs disappeared with a yelp.

'We've caught something feisty!' a voice cried gleefully. 'It's got a nasty scratch on it, ain't it, boys?'

The dogs whimpered. 'That'll teach ya to keep your noses out of places they ain't wanted,' another voice chuckled. 'Be careful. Whatever's inside ain't leavin' quietly.'

Asta jolted backwards, watching two hands clad in brown leather gloves emerge through the leaves and drop a cow-skin coat that reeked of human stench over the trap.

Asta growled bitterly. 'It's a fighter!' sniggered one of the men, digging around the trap.

He wrenched it from the ground and Asta tumbled on her side as the man roughly tugged it into the open air.

'Let's see what we've got ourselves this time.'

The man ripped the leather from the trap and Asta hissed, her fur bristling all over her body.

The men reorganized the muskets on their shoulders and placed the cloth bags bulging with the weight of dead animals on the ground.

'Look at that!' the thin man jeered, crouching on his haunches with the other man and elbowing him in the ribs. The hunters peered into cage and Asta's pupils dilated. 'A live wildcat!'

'Bit small, ain't it?' the stout man commented, reaching for the handle welded to the top of the trap. Asta leaped with a furious slash of her claws. The man jumped, tripped over his feet and landed heavily on his backside.

The thin man hooted with laughter. 'Never underestimate the ferocity of a wildcat!' He caught his breath and wiped a tear from his eye. 'Mad Rathder will pay us a fine sum for this beauty!'

'How are we meant to get this fiend back to London if we can't carry it?' The stout man frowned. 'Are you sure we can't kill it?'

'He asked for a *live* one when we sold him the other wildcat parts, remember?' the thin man retorted. 'Wildcats are rare enough for us to charge what we like, but a *live* one demands a special price.'

'Then that curmudgeon might change his mind altogether. This cat's got the devil in its veins!'

'He won't,' the thin man scoffed. 'He wants a live one so he never runs out of wildcat ingredients. He'll use its whiskers, blood, claws, spit to treat everything from your headaches to gout.'

'He ain't getting near this demon to harvest anything.'

'That ain't our problem.' The thin man shrugged, scanning the forest and pointing to a withered oak tree. 'Go and snap off one of them long branches over there. We can thread it through the handle and carry the cage back to the cart between our shoulders.'

The trap dangled from the middle of the branch with Asta yowling and throwing her body against its solid wrought-iron frame. She hoped to break the bough or snap the handle, but both were solid, and her caterwauling only elicited chuckles from the hunters and slobbering hops of excitement from the dogs.

The humans trudged through the trees until they reached the same grassy corridor Asta recognized from three days before. The men lay the trap on the ground beside their cart and unhooked then rolled back its waxed canvas top. They strained as they lifted Asta, and awkwardly manoeuvred her cage into the back of the wagon. Then they unloaded the rest of their catch and covered them with the canvas, plunging Asta into darkness.

The men's footsteps disappeared into the distance. Asta's eyes flittered about the cart, her blood ringing in her ears as the smell of dead stoat, pheasant, rabbit and crow crept up her nose. The wagon was deep and she was completely sealed inside. Even if she could have reached its edges, she would never be able to topple the cage over the side and smash it like she had hoped.

A jittery feeling of despair swept over her. There was no way out, and each moment that passed brought Asta's fate closer. With a sob rising in her throat, she tucked her limbs into her body and wrapped her thick, blunt tail closely round her. She hid her face behind it, wishing it was Ash's or her mother's fur brushing against her cheek, and thought of all she had lost and everything she feared to come.

CHAPTER FIVE

SURRENDER

Asta had never felt so helpless, so tired, so hungry and so defeated. There was nothing she could do to stop the humans from stealing her away from her home. But she would never be tamed. She would make sure no human ever came near her.

An hour passed before footsteps sounded, and Asta cowered, hearing the hunters' chuckles and the dogs' panting draw near. The canvas top was whipped away and the cart flooded with daylight.

'How's the little baggage up front?' a voice asked. Boxes scraped as they were dragged and shifted about the wagon, and Asta's ears flattened as a broad face peered over the side and gazed into her dilated eyes.

Asta hissed.

'Still here,' the stout man said, unmoved, 'and still just as friendly, but she ain't touched that rabbit.'

'No matter, the weaker and more docile she is, the better,' the thin man replied, groaning as he lifted another branch over the cart with an identical trap dangling from its centre. 'Keep them apart. They could scrap and we don't want to damage our most valuable wares.'

Another scent drifted into the wagon and Asta's head darted towards the creature, growling inside its cage.

'As alike at two peas!' The thin man beamed, pulling the branch free from the other trap. 'I shoulda found these woods years ago. I've never known such booty.'

Asta stood on her hind legs and peered over the crates that separated the cages. She could just see the top of a wildcat, hunched inside its trap. It was spitting at the hunters who ignored it completely.

'Ash?' Asta whispered. 'Ash, is that you?'

The other wildcat stopped snarling. Pricking its ears towards her, it reared up in its cage and stared in her direction. Asta stared into a pair of eyes she'd always known.

'Asta?' Ash blinked in disbelief.

'I thought you were dead!' Asta mewed, yearning to press her head against his.

'Where's Mother?' Ash's voice rasped with worry. 'Did she get away? Is she coming to help us?'

Asta didn't know what to say. The hopeful glint in Ash's eyes choked the words in her throat. Asta bowed her head, her voice smaller than she had ever heard it. 'On that day we were separated, she didn't survive the chase. These hunters shot her and took her away.'

Ash's yellow eyes clouded with sorrow and his face disappeared from view. The silence that followed brought tears to Asta's eyes and her hackles stiffened with hatred, listening to the men count their kills and hoot with triumph as they packed limp animal bodies into the boxes.

'What happened to you?' Asta asked at last, trying to think of anything but the dead animal scents now filling her nose. 'I waited in the den and when you didn't return I looked everywhere for you.'

'When the humans and their dogs came,' Ash began, his voice wavering, 'I sprinted into the woods like you and Mother. I was terrified. I didn't think which direction I was going in. I just ran until my paws couldn't go any further.

'I was too frightened to turn back. I thought you and Mother must be somewhere together, so I hid deep inside an empty rabbit warren. I planned to return to the den when it was safe. I must have fallen asleep, because when I stepped into the forest again, the moon was sinking and the rain had come.

'It was then that I realized how lost I was. Mother had never taken us to that part of the forest before. There were no scents to track nor any

familiar trees or shrubs to guide me. No matter which way I went, I found myself no closer to home. The trees grew thornier and seemed to scowl at me in the shadows, and the sounds of the owls and the foxes screeching in the darkness scared me back to the warren.

'The next morning, I still couldn't find the den. I was so hungry. I tried to hunt, but I didn't catch anything – not even a moth. I followed my nose all day, hoping to catch a scent of you or Mother. That's when I smelled this rabbit. It made me think of home. I never imagined it would trap me in *this*.'

There was a thump as Ash hurled himself against his cage, and Asta's whiskers drooped, feeling the same bite of shame gnaw inside her.

'I called and called, hoping you and Mother would find me,' Ash went on, 'but, when night fell, the owls and the foxes were everywhere again, and I didn't dare make another sound. I willed you and Mother to be alive and free.' He paused to collect himself. 'Yet we all ended up in the same place.'

Asta trembled with grief. She wished everything was different: that they had never left the den with their mother, that she had not argued for them to stay out and hunt, that the men had never discovered their woodland.

'I reckon we sell one of these cats to Mad Rathder, as planned, and claim the Vermin Act on the other,' the stout man suggested, shuffling the last crate into the cart and rolling the canvas top back over the wagon. 'There's a lot more to be earned for its fur and suchlike.'

'These cats aren't fully grown,' the thin man said. 'Their pelts aren't big enough to be valuable. I swear on my musket: Mad Rathder will pay more than we claim from the parish on the Vermin Act and then some. If he's tricky, we'll tell him he can sell their fur when they are fully grown. It's a shrewd investment. He can't argue with that.'

'But he only asked for one wildcat, not two. If he doesn't buy both, then . . .'

'Remember what he was like when he bought the wildcat parts?' the thin man interrupted, his face etched in a scowl. 'He was rubbing his hands with glee! He'll fall over himself for two. And, *if* he doesn't, there'll be another apothecary who'll pay for the other. They're all competitive, miserly, curs that's why Mad Rathder will want *both* cats. It'll give him the advantage over the other apothecaries. He'll control the market on wildcat concoctions and everyone will come to him. So stop your worrying and let's get packed up. It's a six-hour journey at a trot and we want to make it to Mad Rathder before dark.'

'Asta!' Ash howled as the canvas covered the cart and enveloped them in darkness. 'What's happening? Who is Mad Rathder?'

The backboard clanked shut as the men bolted them inside and whistled for the dogs to join them at the front of the cart.

'They're taking us to London.' Asta shivered. 'Do you remember? Mother said it was one of those human cities like an ant's nest. The hunters are selling us to someone called Mad Rathder who uses animal parts to make medicines.'

'Then we have to get out of here!' Ash's voice cracked with panic and he threw himself against the walls of his cage again.

'Ash, stop!' Asta cried. 'You'll hurt yourself. There's no way out!' The sound of his body clashing against metal ceased and Asta's eyes filled with tears, hearing him whimper. 'The humans can't keep us inside these traps forever. Our only hope is to save our strength and attack them as soon as we are freed. Then we'll run as fast as we can back to the forest.'

CHAPTER SIX

TO LONDON

The wagon clattered out of the forest towards the village of Stratfield Mortimer. Its wheels bounced against the uneven grassy track, and Asta and Ash yelped as they stumbled and struck their cages, again and again.

The further they travelled the more the wildcats prickled with unease. Not a day had passed when they hadn't listened to the leaves rustling in the breeze or the birds chirping in the trees. Now all they heard was the horses' strides and the clunk of wood as the cart's cast-iron wheels ground along country roads. By the time the path changed and the horses' hooves began to clop along firmer ground, both wildcats were light-headed with nausea and slumped on their sides, breathing raggedly.

'Whoa, girls!' one of the men ordered, and the horses came to a stop. Asta and Ash's ears twitched weakly, hearing brisk footsteps then three pounding raps. After a pause, a clank sounded, then voices.

'Got us a couple more forest tigers,' the thin man said as he unhooked the canvas top and whipped it open. Asta and Ash were blasted by bright sunshine. Two faces peered down their noses into the cages. The wildcats glared back at them and hissed feebly.

'Why in God's name would you bring them here *alive?*' said a plump man with flushed, shiny cheeks, curling his lips in disgust. 'Kill them at once!'

'An apothecary in London ordered them. Live cats are more valuable to him than dead.'

The ruddy-cheeked man pondered, tapping his chin with a pudgy finger. 'But they are less valuable to me. The Vermin Act states that they must be deceased for a bounty to be claimed. You are bending the rules. I'll give you a penny for each kitten if you insist on taking them alive.'

'You dog!' the thin man snapped. 'You gave us a shilling for the last one and there's two here.'

'The previous wildcat was *dead*. She was a fine specimen – a true predator and a threat to our local poultry houses. But these are not full-grown. They are weak and thin – more likely to perish than prey upon another creature. I suspect the first wildcat you brought was their mother.'

'Then she was more valuable than a shilling. We saved the poultry houses *and* prevented two more killers prowling through your parish.' There was a long pause as the churchwarden and the thin man stared defiantly at one another. 'Sixpence each,' the thin man said through gritted teeth. 'A shilling in total.'

'*Thruppence* each and that's my final word on two *live* wildcat kittens, or you can consider your excursion to my door as a complete waste of time.'

The thin man sighed in defeat and stomped to the butt of the wagon. He furiously opened the backboard and roughly dragged and opened the boxes for inspection. The churchwarden scribbled the name of each dead animal in a little notebook, and when there was nothing else to view, he retrieved a leather pouch from his pocket. It jingled as it flew through the air into the thin man's grasp. The churchwarden turned and walked away. The hunter greedily ripped it open and counted each coin in his palm. He shoved the money into his pocket and muttered curses as he covered the wagon with the canvas once more.

The onward journey to London along the Devil's Highway was long and uncomfortable.

Asta and Ash shared their fears for the future. Each

time Ash grew quiet, Asta encouraged him to help her plot their escape, but, as the hours passed, his increasing stillness frightened her. If his spirit faded, everything could be lost, and they would need all their courage to flee the human world.

'Ash, we must eat something,' she said at last, trying to ignore the queasiness griping in her gut. 'Food will make us stronger.'

'I can't, Asta.' Ash shook his head weakly.

'We haven't eaten for three days,' Asta urged. 'We won't have the strength to get out of here if we fast for much longer.'

There was a pause. Ash groaned, knowing she was right.

Swallowing was difficult at first. They were too grief-stricken and afraid to stomach food, but over the next few hours they forced down small mouthfuls, and in time their nausea eased and drowsiness followed as the rock of the wagon grew smoother.

The wildcats drifted into a dark sleep. Neither had ever been awake for this long. They were used to lazing during the day and saving their energy for dawn and dusk hunts with their mother. They both slept fitfully, the unusual sounds, and the smells of the dead forest animals, polluting their dreams with dread.

It was the rank odour of human filth that eventually roused them. A sour, stinking vapour of smoke, rotting food and bodily waste seeped into the cart. To breathe was to smell, and they spluttered in a bid to rid the foulness in their nostrils. They tucked their faces into their bodies, preferring to stifle themselves on their own fur than suffer the rancid air. Within an hour, the wagon floundered on its wheels once more, and bumped and ground along uneven stone roads, throwing the wildcats against their cages again, their tender bruises flaring with each new strike.

The strange noises of the city terrified them. Their instincts craved to see what danger lurked nearby. Their eyes searched the cart, yet they saw nothing but its contents rocking from side to side. The taut canvas top made them blind to the threats clanging and shouting outside. Their imaginations swelled with each man-made bang and rattle, and every sudden human cackle and yell or dog bark turned into a nightmarish assault they had no way of escaping.

The cart veered down streets and alleyways, and Asta's and Ash's heartbeats began to slow as they left the hubbub behind and listened to the regular clip of horse's hooves. The early evening sun, sinking behind the towering buildings, cast the roads in shadow, and Asta and Ash breathed easier as the oppressive warmth inside the wagon began to subside.

The cart made one last turn and halted. 'A delivery for the eminent Rathder!' one of the hunters called in a grand voice that made the other man snigger. A series of thuds followed as they dismounted the wagon with the two dogs sniffing vigorously at their surroundings.

'You open up the boxes while I do the talking,' the first man whispered. 'We'll shift these cats and see what other parts we can trade, then we'll go to a tavern to celebrate.'

A fresh wave of fear surged through the wildcats. They had arrived at Mad Rathder's Apothecary Shop.

There was a creak and the sound of footsteps striding quickly towards them.

'Have you found what I asked?' a nasal voice asked with an excited chuckle.

'Nothing but prime specimens from the best forests to the west!'

The canvas top whipped open. Asta and Ash blanched as their gazes roved wildly over strange black-and-white buildings looming down at them on all sides, with windows like staring eyes. Directly over their heads, a carved wooden tablet of a pestle and mortar hung beside another, newer, sign of a sun, surrounded by twelve symbols and a mixture of animals and humans. Below it, a double door was left ajar between two large bay windows made up of small, latticed squares of glass.

A pale, weathered face leered into the cart and goggled at the wildcats. The man's shiny, balding head domed from a hoop of long white hair, scattered in disarray around his ears. A long, grey, unkempt beard twitched slightly around his mouth as his cold stare travelled over the wildcats. Asta and Ash stared up at him and growled.

'Kittens? *Two* of them?' Rathder uttered incredulously. 'This isn't what I requested!'

'If you're keeping them alive to harvest their parts for your medicines,' the thin man spoke, folding his arms over the wagon as the stout man uncovered the rest of the boxes, filled with dead animals, 'they'll need time to recover after you've extracted whatever you've needed. When you harvest one, the other will be fit enough to harvest something more. And, if you tire of them, you can sell their fur, once they're fully grown. What you have here is a sound, long-term investment.'

Rathder stared at Asta and Ash, his thin lips scrunching as ideas rolled through his mind.

'I hear there's a big, new apothecary opening on Thames Street,' the thin man sneered. Rathder's nostrils flared. 'But it won't be a patch on your trade. You'll rule the market with two live wildcats at your disposal for potions. It'll make you famous and you'll be able to meet *double* the demand from customers.'

'And double the cost to feed and maintain two of them,' Rathder added, chewing the inside of his cheek. 'They'll also take up twice the space.'

'If you're not interested,' the thin man sighed, standing upright and giving the stout man a nod to cover up the boxes in the back of the cart, 'there's another apothecary we know who'd like them.'

'No!' Rathder snapped and the other men smiled wryly. 'They're mine!'

At that moment, a woman's face appeared beside Rathder and peered into the back of the cart. She was about fifty years old and her mousey-brown hair was tied back in a neat bun. Her face was fair and even when she frowned the lines around her bright blue eyes seemed to smile. A large raven was perched on her shoulder, and its ebony gaze followed hers as they travelled over the wagon's contents. On seeing the boxes piled with dead animals, her face clouded with sadness, and as her eyes met Asta's, staring up at her through the iron mesh of her cage, the woman gasped.

'Those are forest tigers!' she cried. 'Young, *wild* creatures!'

'Get away from our wagon, you nosey hag!' the stout

man interrupted, shooing her away with his arms as though she was an animal herself.

'You've torn them from their home!' she went on indignantly, ignoring him. 'How could you?'

'We're salesmen delivering our wares, little hen,' the thin hunter said in a silvery tone that immediately hardened the woman's jaw. 'If you're not an interested customer, then our business ain't any concern of yours.'

'If this woman has her way, she will put a stop to your business altogether,' said Rathder, 'she takes great pleasure in destroying the livelihoods of men like us. She believes animals have feelings.' He scoffed. 'Many a hunter, apothecary and gambler has suffered because of her.'

The men eyed one another nervously.

'Marcus Rathder, is this your doing?' The woman whirled on the apothecary. He retreated from her, his shoulders bunching around his ears. '*Live* wildcats?' she went on, shadowing his steps. 'They're elusive, solitary, woodland creatures. They will die a slow and miserable death in a city.'

Ignoring her, Rathder quickened his pace. He clicked his fingers and urgently motioned for the hunters to take the two cages inside his shop.

The men leaped into action. They lifted Asta and Ash's cages into the air by the tree branch and the wildcats hissed as they stumbled against the sway. The hunters stretched it between their shoulders and strode towards the entrance to the apothecary shop where Rathder now stood, holding the double doors wide open for them.

The woman pointed into the cages. 'Look at these cats – they are terrified!'

The men paid no attention to her protests. She turned to the hunters. 'Name your price,' she implored, gently placing her hand on the stout man's arm. '*I* will buy them from you.'

'We don't deal with busybodies!' The stout man shot out his leg in a violent kick that smashed against her knee.

The wildcats flinched as the woman cried out in pain. She tumbled heavily upon the cobbled stones. The raven cawed in alarm and burst into the air.

Rathder's door swung shut and a heavy thud sounded as it was bolted from inside. The raven landed beside the woman and paced anxiously as she drew a sharp breath and peeled herself from the ground.

She stood unsteadily and glowered at the apothecary shop before limping away, with her raven protectively circling the air above her and squawking in disgust.

CHAPTER SEVEN

RATHDER'S
APOTHECARY SHOP

The two hunters stood in the middle of Rathder's shop floor, with Asta and Ash dangling in their cages from the middle of the tree branch. The wildcats' eyes flickered over the room. Drawers and bunches of dried poppy bulbs and herbs hung from tall shelves that were crammed to the ceiling with books, rows of coloured bottles, boxes and cups. Assorted ceramic pots were labelled with strange ingredients, scrawled in spidery, black handwriting, such as **DEVIL'S BREATH, MUMIA, FROG'S LUNGS, KING'S DROPS, UNICORN HORN, LEECHES** and **CRAB'S EYES**.

Rathder scurried past them into the depths of the room where a stuffed alligator, a turtle and three inflated blowfishes hung from rafters painted indigo with gold stars and planets. A long oak counter spanned the width of the shop floor.

Behind it, a cauldron bubbled above
a fire in a hearth beside a table covered
with a mixture of distilling flasks. They were
filled with different levels of liquids in various
hues that dripped and steamed as chemical

reactions morphed into medical remedies for Rathder to sell.

Asta and Ash gazed fearfully around the strange human place. Everything crowded their senses with peril, yet there was no way of escaping, and each breath they drew was thick with unfamiliar scents that filled them with dread.

'Bring my pretties over here.' Rathder grinned wolfishly, hurriedly pushing aside earthenware slabs, bowls, jars, a brass pestle and mortar and a large set of scales.

The objects clinked as they moved across the counter. The hunters awkwardly manoeuvred Asta's and Ash's cages upon it, and Rathder dipped his head to drink them in. His face smouldered with ambition and a determined smile drew across his lips.

'We'll be leaving now, Rathder,' the thin man said pointedly, withdrawing the tree branch from the cages. 'We've got the rest of our haul to sell.'

Rathder stood upright, fiddled with the set of keys jangling at his hip and disappeared through a doorway in the corner of the room. He reappeared a few moments later with a British blue cat that slunk inside and trotted beside his ankles.

'A crown,' he said, scratching the silver coin flat across the counter towards the men with a bony finger. The hunters' jaws slackened. Neither had expected such a sum. The thin man reached out his hand, but Rathder quickly drew the silver coin back with a flick of his finger. 'And that pays for your silence.'

'We guarantee it –' the thin man gave a nod – 'but I can't say the same about that woman outside.'

'Pah! I'm not worried about Miriam.' Rathder released the coin. 'She's a Dutch immigrant, who inherited her husband's estate. He was a criminal, killed trying to free baiting bears from the Hope Theatre ten years ago. One of Culpeper's protégés, a traitor to physicians and apothecaries. No one of any rank takes her seriously.'

His cat leaped on to the counter and sniffed the cages with a pretty silvery-blue nose. Asta and Ash's eyes pored over the domestic cat, which was so like them, yet so different. But the cat was as indifferent as a sphinx and calmly sat on her haunches with her paws placed neatly in front of her. She blinked adoringly at her master. He stroked her from top to tail, and she purred loudly and lifted herself to press her head against his hand.

'My Beauty, my darling girl,' Rathder cooed, scratching the cat under her chin.

'We need our traps back now, if you please,' the thin man added impatiently, swiftly pocketing the money.

'Blacksmith made them for us, especially.'

'Of course,' the apothecary replied, crouching below the counter and digging out a roll of canvas. He hummed contentedly as he cast it over the cages as if he was covering a table with cloth.

Asta and Ash stared at one another, their eyes round with terror.

'What's happening?' Ash whispered.

Asta hurried to him and pressed her body against her cage, wishing she could feel his warmth against hers. 'I don't know.' She shook her head, desperation furrowing her brow.

'I'm scared, Asta,' Ash whimpered, shuffling closer to her.

'Me too.' Asta swallowed the lump swelling in her throat, wanting to be strong for her brother. They winced, hearing Rathder's high-pitched whistle grate in their ears as he opened and closed drawers, clinked glasses, ground powders and poured liquids into a concoction they could not see. Asta bared her claws, trying to summon her courage. 'As soon as they open these cages, we have to fly at them with all our strength, then we must run out of this place as fast as we can.'

Ash nodded, his desperate face mirroring hers. Just then,

a hand abruptly appeared between the cages. Before they could react, it had vanished, leaving behind a small bowl, swirling with a sweet, musky vapour, smelling of wet dirt and fish.

Someone quickly patted the heavy canvas down, trapping the smoke inside, and Asta and Ash spluttered as a cloying, bitter taste invaded their nostrils and throats. The mist swiftly parched their mouths and scratched their eyes. Asta and Ash thrashed about in their cages in panic, but all too soon a heady blur took hold and the wildcats crumpled on their sides. They yearned to call out for each other, but neither could utter a sound.

A moment later, the wildcats tumbled headlong into darkness.

Asta dragged her eyes open and blinked away the deep, unnatural sleep that lingered on her eyelids. She squinted against a warm, bright light and her ears twitched towards birdsong and soft metallic clangs she had not heard before. Her head swam with the horrors of the previous day, and she slowly lifted her body upright with trembling legs. The top of her tail throbbed under a bandage that was blotched with dried blood, and something cold and heavy weighed down round her neck. She scratched it with her hind leg, but the steel collar hardly moved.

'Ash?' she mewed, her voice strangled into a croaking whisper. A barb of worry tightened in her chest, seeing his terrified face flash in her memory. 'Ash?'

Asta blinked, urging her eyes to focus against the glare. The summer sunshine was pouring into a room through a pair of latticed windows. The lead-framed diamonds of glass caged the view of a small garden that was overshadowed by other buildings beneath the clear morning sky. She sighed heavily, yearning to be back in the forest where she used to watch the familiar green leaves of the forest flutter against the blue.

She searched for Ash, her gaze flicking over boxes and chests stacked against panelled walls with twelve painted wall hangings of animals, stars, burning comets and planets above pastoral scenes. Scrolls were also pinned to the walls and depicted elongated drawings of women in profile whose heads were those of cats.

She backed into her cage and shivered with terror. A tall figure wearing a wide-brimmed hat was standing in the corner of the room. It looked like a mutated man. It was broad, with oily, waxy brown skin, a baggy face and unblinking thick disks for eyes. A long beak protruded for a nose and huge hands hung by its sides. Asta hunched low, watching a bluebottle land on the monster's forehead, scurry down its face and scuttle across its eyeballs. Asta held her breath, waiting for the monster to bat the insect away, but it remained completely still, and the drumming of her heart slowed as she realized this strange presence was not alive.

Breathing easier, Asta dared to look about the room again. A telescope and an enormous globe of the world stood beside shelves overflowing with books and papers, whole crabs' shells, and dead frogs, lizards and snakes preserved in glass jars filled with yellowing fluid. A birdcage on legs stood in front of them, with six blackbirds gently trilling and whistling or hopping along perches that softly jangled with every bounce. None would meet Asta's eye. They fluttered closer to one another and whispered nervously as Beauty, the British blue cat, languidly bathed in the sunlight below. She reclined against another wrought-iron cage that was exactly like Asta's on the other side of the room. Ash was inside it, facing away from her and lying on his side. His ears cocked towards Beauty, who was purring soothing words that Asta could not hear.

A protective growl rose in her throat. 'Ash?'

Beauty slowly blinked in Asta's direction. 'Awake at last.' Beauty smiled and her intense copper gaze met Asta's bright green stare. 'Eat and drink something. It will make you feel better. My master has given you food and water in those bowls beside you.'

Asta tensed. She didn't want to speak to this human pet. She wanted Ash to respond, but he only adjusted his head and stared into space. His eyes were dull and sad. Asta stepped forward, trying to get closer to him, but she swayed dizzily. Her sense of space felt different and unbalanced.

'Don't worry.' Beauty yawned indifferently. 'They grow back in time.'

Asta lifted her paw and grazed it across her face. Some of her whiskers on her cheeks and above her eyes had been trimmed.

'You have both been chosen for a very noble purpose,' Beauty said, stretching her front legs ahead of her before standing on four paws. She nuzzled her head against the corner of Ash's cage and padded towards Asta. 'There's no need to fear my master.' She sat on her haunches before Asta and peered down her nose at her with a regal air. 'He is a healer. He cures human illnesses and you and your brother have the ability to help him do that. Your blood and whiskers have special powers.'

Asta glowered at Beauty, disgusted that she was subservient to a human being. 'We do not want to help the humans,' Asta growled. 'We belong in our forest. We want to go home.'

'But you *are* home,' Beauty said matter-of-factly. She walked alongside Asta's cage and rubbed her cheek and the length of her body against its metal frame. Asta recoiled as Beauty's scent filled the small, enclosed space. 'And you are far safer here than in your forest – you're both nearly starved and you've seen what those dangerous hunters are capable of,' Beauty added, strolling back to Ash with her tail in the air. Asta's jaw clenched. 'Now you're here, you'll never have to worry like that again. I will protect you. You are both part of our family now and we help each other whenever we can. You'll soon forget your forest. You're lucky we rescued you from it when we did.'

Beauty blinked and gazed wistfully at Ash. His ears were fixed towards her silky tones.

Asta's ears flattened. She could see the fight going out of her brother. They had to escape before it was too late.

CHAPTER EIGHT

BEAUTY

Asta longed to speak to Ash alone, but Beauty was never far away. Even when the cat slept, she seemed to wake as soon as Asta and Ash started whispering to one another, and when Asta slumbered, she often stirred to the sound of Beauty's soft voice speaking gently, offering to help the wildcats in whatever ways she could. She urged them to build up their strength and eat the cuts of meat Rathder slipped into their cages each evening. After three days Asta ate the food, but it wasn't for Beauty's benefit. Every mouthful she chewed was to energize their escape and she hoped Ash was doing the same.

The wildcats had been imprisoned for two weeks when Beauty and Ash began resting side by side, pressing their flanks against the mesh of his cage. Asta felt a stab of betrayal seeing him seek the warmth of someone else, and she felt lonelier than ever, having no one to curl up to on the opposite side of the room. She had not felt the touch of another since the morning they lost their mother, and she longed to be near Ash again. He was her only friend in the world.

Beauty befriended him in every way she could. She playfully rolled on to her back and blinked slowly and softly at him with her gleaming copper eyes. Beauty interrupted every conversation Asta had with him about their forest and reminded them how lucky they were to be safe from the dangers of the wild, how there was no need to fear their new home and their human master, who was protecting them from the evils of the world that would strike the moment they left his care.

'Our master is a selfless man,' she would purr, her gaze warmly flitting between the wildcats as she lounged beside Ash's cage in the sunshine. 'Last year a terrifying pestilence raged through the streets of London. It tortured and killed almost every person it touched. The king, his court and almost every doctor in the city fled, leaving the rest of its citizens to face their fate alone. Our master didn't, though,' she added, pride twinkling all over her face. 'He stayed and risked his life to help the sick and gave them medicine to ease the pain. He treated my dear human family before they died from the sickness too. He was merciful and brought them peace.' Her brow creased with sadness. 'I thought I would be alone forever before Rathder found me. Loneliness is the most terrible feeling.' Beauty paused, her expression darkening. 'But I still wasn't safe. The disease was unstoppable and the humans needed someone to blame.' Her voice cracked. 'Like you, I was also hunted by men.'

A sigh shuddered from Beauty's lips and Ash edged towards her, his head sympathetically tilting to one side. Asta listened, a pang of pity rising within her, remembering the horror of being chased through the forest by the hunters and watching them steal her mother away.

'All the cats and dogs in the city were rounded up to stop the spread.' Beauty sniffed. 'They say two hundred thousand cats and forty thousand dogs were murdered. Brutes pounded on our master's door and pushed their way inside this room in search of me. But our master was too clever for them. He put me in a cage and hid me inside the skirts of his plague suit over there.' She gestured her head to the sinister, beaked figure, lifelessly staring at them from the corner of the room. 'They didn't want to come near because they knew my master wore it to treat the sick. I detested the cage, just like you hate yours, but it saved me from those cruel men who roam outside these walls. If you behave, he will free you too.'

Asta bristled. 'Why can't he release us now?'

'Because he knows you will try to escape.' Beauty stared back. 'And, if you do, the thugs in the streets outside will beat you to death like those poor other cats and dogs. Most humans are not kind to animals. That's why you must stay here. My master and I can protect you from harm, but we can't give you the freedom to roam around the house until we know you have accepted us and your new home.'

Asta's and Ash's eyes met across the room. If only there was a way for them to speak to one another without Beauty, then Asta would know what Ash was really thinking. Asta clenched her jaw, her mind consumed by thoughts of returning to their forest, but to Asta's alarm Ash turned to the cat, brimming with affection and trust.

Beauty watched Asta closely, twitching the tip of her tail. 'Do you see those scrolls over there with the pictures of women with cat's heads?' she said, trotting over to the nearby shelves and leaping upon them. The blackbirds trilled nervously in their cages as she slunk between a human skull and various jars to sit beside the illustrations. 'That's Bastet –' she lifted her paw and smiled proudly – 'an Egyptian goddess that shields homes from evil spirits. The ancient Egyptians believed cats were good omens. Our master sees you and me in the same way.' Beauty stared at the wildcats with a soft, ingratiating smile. 'He is not our adversary. He is our friend who respects us as much as we should respect him.'

Beauty elegantly hopped to the floor and sprang across the floorboards to Ash's cage. She coquettishly rubbed her body against it, before she flittered to Asta's cage to do the same.

'Our master has grand plans.' She laughed musically and pounced into the space between the wildcats, and reclined neatly with a wistful stare into the distance. 'One day, he will earn enough riches to transport us from this inner city shack to a beautiful house, surrounded by rich walled gardens, where we will be safe from the hooligans that fill the streets of London. We'll spend our days catching birds and butterflies; we'll climb the leafiest trees.' She smiled, a purr rising in her throat. She glanced at Asta, then Ash, and blinked at him sweetly. 'Together, we'll help a good man like our master achieve all the glory he deserves.'

Asta's tail flicked. She wasn't convinced that a man who could pluck two wildcats from their home, drug them and use their blood and whiskers for medical use was as noble as Beauty would have them believe.

And, no matter how hard Beauty tried to persuade

them, Asta would never forget her forest, where she and Ash belonged.

Rathder administered the sleeping smoke every Friday at dusk. Beauty hurried to him whenever he entered the room at the back of the building where the wildcats were stored. She weaved around his ankles as he approached the wildcats' cages with two rolls of thick canvas under his arms and two bowls stacked on top of the other. Ash was always the first to be anaesthetized, but before the canvas shrouded his cage Beauty would rub her head against it and mew softly to allay his fears and to praise him for helping those in need.

Rathder dropped the heavy material over Ash and slipped a bowl, whirling with sweet, earthy smoke beneath it. With Beauty trotting beside him, he stepped towards Asta, who shrank into the depths of her cage. Beauty offered Asta no words of comfort like she did for Ash. She sat on her haunches and coldly watched Asta's hackles rise.

Again and again, the wildcats rose to fewer blackbirds singing in their cages, and fresh cuts on their tails where they had been bled. Yet as the weeks passed, Ash padded willingly towards Beauty and Rathder, who affectionately smacked his lips together each time Ash neared. But Asta could never hide her unease, and Beauty's pupils dilated with delight, watching Asta quail each time Rathder came near.

With Beauty never leaving Ash's side, Asta had no way of telling him how Beauty glowered at her when they were alone, and despair soon crept into Asta's heart. She retreated into herself and spent her days curled up in a ball with her back turned to the room. She responded less and less, and slept more and more, preferring to escape the misery and loneliness of the waking world.

Beauty nestled beside Ash and whispered to him not to worry, and as she stared at Asta across the room a soft, self-satisfied smile drew across her lips, knowing Asta's spirit was fading.

The wildcats had been held captive for six weeks when Asta roused to the sound of Ash speaking softly into her ear and pressing his head against hers through the wrought-iron mesh of her cage. It was a morning after the wildcats had been drugged and bled, and once again the sleeping smoke had made Asta weak and queasy. It had been so long since she had felt his touch that at first she thought she was dreaming of their den in the forest, and she purred.

'Let her sleep,' Asta heard Beauty mew. Asta woke with

a start, the cold realization of where she really was stabbing her like a bite to the face. 'She doesn't want to talk to you.'

'Please don't go,' Asta pleaded, feeling him withdraw. She snapped her head up in search of him, and her eyes widened with surprise, finding him sitting on his haunches beside Beauty on the other side of her cage. It was quieter than normal, and when Asta turned to the blackbirds' cage she realized the last one had disappeared. She sighed, knowing it had met its fate in Rathder's hands.

'Are you all right?' Ash asked, bending his pink nose to hers.

'How did you get out?' Asta briskly stood up and looked at his cage. His door was open, meaning he was free to come and go from it as he pleased.

'He earned our master's trust.' Beauty spoke for him in a self-satisfied tone that made the fur along Asta's spine stiffen. 'Ash knows he is safer and happier here with me than he ever was in that forest of yours.' The cat nuzzled into Ash's neck. 'We were destined to find each other. It was written in the stars.'

Asta's jaw dropped watching Ash rub his cheek against Beauty's and smile. She couldn't believe how close they had become. She wondered what Beauty must have been whispering into his ear all this time, what she must have said to convince him to forget his home and want to stay with her as a pet with her villainous human master. She had to get him away from here as soon as she could.

'What do you mean it was written in the stars?' Asta tried to sound as friendly as possible so Beauty would not have another reason to treat her with disdain.

'Do you remember the bright, burning star we saw the night before Mother died?' Ash asked.

'Yes.' Asta nodded. 'Mother said they brought about great change.'

'Our master and I saw it too.' Beauty smiled, her eyes travelling over the twelve wall hangings of planets, comets and astrological symbols placed around the room. 'He is a star reader, and he predicted Ash would come to me. The falling star made it so. It was fate that brought us together.'

'I remember it,' Asta mewed softly, bowing her head submissively. If she appeared defeated, perhaps Beauty would think she had also accepted her life as a pet. 'Please let me out of this cage. I want to stay here with you too,' Asta lied. 'It isn't safe for us back in the forest.' The untruth made Beauty's face flare with impatience.

Beauty turned to Ash. 'How can I trust her when she's whispered such unkind things to me while you have been asleep?' Beauty pathetically furrowed her brow and Ash's face fell at once. He stared at Asta and his ears flattened. He clearly believed everything Beauty said.

A low growl festered in Asta's throat at the injustice, but she suppressed it, knowing Beauty was trying to poison Ash's mind. If she didn't react the way Beauty wanted, Beauty wouldn't have power over her.

'I want to be friends, Beauty,' Asta offered, the false words burning her tongue as she did her best to sound sincere. 'It's hard being caged when we have been used to the wild. Please let me go and I will prove it to you. I won't run away. I wouldn't dare to go outside after everything you have saved us from. I want to stay here with you and our master.'

Beauty and Asta's eyes met. In the silence that followed, a wry smile drew across the cat's grey face.

'Very well,' Beauty said, her eyes glowing, 'I'll see what I can do.'

CHAPTER NINE

THE BARTHOLOMEW FAIR

Every waking minute, Asta buried her desire to escape and pretended she wanted to stay in Beauty's world. When Beauty spoke, Asta pricked her ears and smiled. When Beauty neared her cage, Asta padded closer to her, and when Ash and Beauty rolled about the floor and entwined their tails and basked in the sunshine together, Asta squashed her alarm and watched them with a contented expression that she hoped masked the sound of her heart clamouring behind her ribs.

Ash was oblivious. He happily spent his days meeting Beauty's cheek rubs and nose dabs with equal affection. Whenever he approached Asta's cage, Beauty gaily leaped upon him and drew him away, somersaulting him across the room. Asta stifled her hurt at those moments and calmed the anger rising inside her by softly closing her eyes and picturing the leaves rustling in the breeze in the forest. Her need to speak to Ash tightened her throat with sadness, but she knew the only way she could talk to him alone was to win Beauty's trust by bowing to her dominance and ignoring every barb the cat spat her way.

Two weeks later, after another night of drugging and bleeding, Asta's green eyes groggily fluttered open against the first soft rays of sunlight and spied something unusual. Her cage door was ajar. She shot her head up from the ground and blinked, clearing her eyes of sleep. She glanced about the room. Nothing else had changed. Ash was slumbering inside his crate as usual, with Beauty reclining just outside his door, which was also open.

Asta's blood thumped. She lightly edged forward, wanting to dash from the prison that had trapped her for two months, but her eyes flitted to Beauty, sleeping peacefully on her side. Asta reminded herself that all her efforts to persuade Beauty that she would not escape would be undone if Asta did anything out of turn. If Asta failed, she could lose Ash to the human world forever.

Asta tiptoed into the middle of the room. It felt enormous after being trapped in the cage for so long. She hunched low and instinctively scanned for an exit, but the only way out was through the latched door in the corner of the room. Asta stared up at the large window to her right and her heart fluttered seeing the white clouds ambling across the blue. She tentatively stretched her limbs, willing their strength to return after so many weeks of only pacing back and forth. Then, craning her neck, she rocketed upwards, and elation rushed through her as she landed on the windowsill with barely a sound.

She peered through the diamonds of glass, longing to feel a breath of fresh air against her fur, and stared into a small garden at the rear of the house. It was framed on either side by tall brick walls that overlooked two long, rectangular grass beds, tangled haphazardly with wilted plants and herbs. Between the beds, a narrow path that was overrun with weeds ran towards a low stone wall that

separated Rathder's property from a broad street.

The first coaches and carts of the morning were wheeling past, and Asta gazed out at a forest of houses on the other side of the road that jettied outward the taller they grew. Tiled roofs, chimney stacks and distant church spires stretched higher than the loftiest trees. Some windows opened as servants emptied full chamber pots on to the street, while others remained closed with their curtains still drawn from the night before.

What struck Asta the most was the absence of colour. All the buildings were whitewashed and had dark brown timbers arranged vertically like bars of a cage, or in curved or triangular patterns within the daub. Except for Rathder's small garden, she could see no green grass or leaves, no yellows, pinks or blues of petals, or red or purple berries. Nothing was wild and alive like Asta was used to. Everything was controlled for human needs.

Asta's ears pricked, hearing the low bellows of cattle approach. A moment later, a drove of oxen walked past, followed by men whipping their haunches. The leather thread cracked in the air as it licked the oxen's hides, and Asta flinched, listening to the poor animals moan.

It was as Asta turned away that she realized she was being watched. Above her, a raven was perched on the wall to her left. It met her gaze with a tilt of its head and an inquisitive blink of its dark eyes, but as soon as Asta started in surprise, it spread its ebony wings and vanished over the rooftops. At the same time, Beauty jumped up on the windowsill and sat beside her.

'Pay no notice to that bird,' Beauty said coldly. 'It belongs to a local busybody. A Dutch woman who harasses our master and steals customers from him.'

Asta resisted the urge to smile. She liked this woman for making Rathder struggle.

Beauty regarded the oxen through the window. 'There's no need to pity them. They are stupid slaves farmed for their meat. Thousands of them are brought from the fields into London for slaughter every week.' Beauty yawned indifferently. 'Then they are chopped into pieces and sold to humans for food at Smithfield Market, not far from here.'

Asta baulked, shocked by Beauty's callous attitude.

A bitter growl rumbled in Beauty's throat. 'Wipe that outraged expression off your face.' She cuffed Asta, her claws raking the skin beneath Asta's right eye. Asta gasped and buried her fury at once, not doubting for a moment that Beauty could snatch away her freedom whenever she wanted. 'You should be grateful the humans feed on beef rather than on you or me. They still eat cats during a famine.' Her copper gaze flashed with pleasure, seeing Asta's eyes round. 'They say we taste like rabbit.'

'Is that true?' Ash mewed, his ears flattening as he joined them on the windowsill. Asta and Ash shivered. They would never savour rabbit in the same way again.

'I won't let anything happen to you,' Beauty purred, rubbing her cheek against his. 'As long as we stay here with our master, we're safe. Every human outside these walls is dangerous, especially to wild animals like you.'

Ash stared at Asta. 'Thank goodness we're here.' Ash's forehead creased earnestly. 'Look how powerful humans are.' His eyes wandered about the room and the streets beyond the window. 'They cut down trees to make houses, they enslave animals for food, they can read the future in the stars and make potions to make them stronger when they are weak. We would never have survived in the forest when humans pursue us so. We're lucky to have been chosen to live with a benevolent master when every other human would have killed us.'

Ash and Beauty looked upon the oxen passing ahead and entwined their tails. Asta's hackles rose. Those were not Ash's words. Beauty's deceit had instilled fear in his mind. How could he not see that they were slaves themselves, imprisoned by a human who was harvesting their blood and whiskers for his own gain? Asta swallowed. It was going to be much harder for her to convince him to escape than she had thought.

With the last straggling oxen, indignant shouts sounded, and the cattle herds whirled round, finding that a large group of horse-drawn wagons and carts, carrying brightly coloured fabrics, long poles and stacks of boxes, had crept up behind them.

'Move those stinking bovines!' a gruff man blustered, roughly pulling his horses' reins as they shuffled uneasily behind the livestock. 'We've got to get to the Bartholomew Fair!'

'Yell all you like,' a young farmhand chuckled, knowing there was little he could do. 'These stubborn beasts don't care where you're going.'

'This happens every year,' Beauty said, unmoved by the increasing commotion. 'The Bartholomew Fair is an annual two-week gathering, trading vice and spectacle. Few humans can resist witnessing its delights and curiosities. London's roads always get blocked whenever it arrives; some of the streets are too narrow.'

The wildcats were transfixed as a crowd of carriages quickly gathered behind the farmers and the oxen. The slower they moved, the more purple-faced the drivers became. Then, as the jam halted, the hollering, cursing and bellowing of the cattle crescendoed into a boisterous furore that drew spectators to their windows, all over the street.

A cluster of carts, carrying a menagerie of caged creatures, came to a standstill in front of Rathder's small garden. Asta and Ash shuddered, their eyes travelling over the imprisoned animals squirming uncomfortably inside their tiny cells. Rats of all sizes and cockerels of all colours were stacked on top of each other in timber crates as though they were vegetables on their way to market. Larger cages housed scratching badgers, squealing swine and barking dogs, but what followed them made the wildcats' whiskers droop on their cheeks the most. Inside a square enclosure was a brown mother bear, sitting on her backside and bowing her head to her cub, burying its face into her stomach.

'The humans pit animals against each other for sport at the fair,' Beauty said. 'These creatures will fight to the death in an arena surrounded by men betting on the bloody outcome. Those animals ahead of you are living proof of the peril you are in.' Asta and Ash stared at the prisoners, their ears flattening. 'People come to my master from all over the city and ask him to predict the winners, but even the stars cannot reveal the champion. It is brains or brawn that wins in the baiting ring.'

It was then that Asta spied a broad figure pushing his way through the throng, his deep-set eyes greedily drinking in the cages. The carriages picked up speed, and he jogged beside them with his head darting between each animal. Swivelling suddenly on his heel, he swerved towards the bear. She roared in alarm and swiped her vast paws. The man stumbled backwards in fright and landed heavily against the street on his bottom. The carriage drivers glided past and hooted with laughter. A scarlet rage rushed into the man's face. Leaping on to his feet, he hurled himself into the front of a cart and struck a guffawing coachman with his fist. The wildcats gasped as the cart wheeled out of sight.

A moment later, the man strode back into view, storming against the flow of traffic to Rathder's low garden wall. He ignored the small gate and sprang over the wall, crushing a bedraggled lavender plant with his boots. Asta and Ash cowered as he stormed up the garden path towards the back door, which was situated beside the window. His jaw was stiff and his cheeks were ruddy.

'Rathder!' the man boomed, walloping the wooden door with his fist. The three cats flinched on the windowsill. 'You old, antiquated rogue – let me in!' Silence followed, and he impatiently pounded the door again. 'Rathder! I know you're there! Get down here, now!'

Asta dared to press her head against the window to stare at him. His back was turned, and his ear was pressed against the door. Beads of sweat dampened the nape of his neck, and his shirt collar was grubby. Asta, Ash and Beauty glanced up as Rathder's footsteps creaked across the floorboards above and clattered down the stairs. The man lunged for the window and cupped his hands round his face as he glared through the glass in frustration. Up close, he was terrifying. The cats hissed as his eyes rounded at the sight of Asta and Ash on the windowsill. All three fled, their fur stiffening all over their bodies.

'Who is that?' Ash trembled, hiding under a table with Beauty and Asta.

The man pounded on the door again. 'Cornelius Moore,' Beauty whispered. 'He's our master's silent business partner. They fought in the Civil Wars together against the Crown.'

'I'm coming!' Rathder grumbled from within.

A moment later, the door creaked open. 'Live wildcats, Rathder?' Moore asked, his voice dulled through the wall.

'No, no, just big tabbies, my friend,' Rathder laughed, insincerity oozing from his throat.

'You don't fool me, *friend*,' Moore rebuffed. The back door thudded shut, and the wildcats' ears pricked, listening eagerly to their muffled conversation. 'I've known you and your tricks for too long.'

'Come, come, Cornelius,' Rathder simpered nervously. 'We're comrades, there's no need for—'

'You and I have debts to repay!' Moore spat. 'The moneylenders will string us up by our necks if we do not deliver something soon. How much have you earned with your new astrology venture?'

'I-I-I have some regular clients,' Rathder stuttered. 'As you know, it takes time for word of mouth to spread . . .'

'If you have been using what pittance we have to indulge yourself with new pets you cannot afford,' Moore growled, 'I'll come down on you so hard you'll think the plague was a birthday present.'

There was a pause as Moore's threat hung in the air.

'They are not pets.' Rathder cleared his throat, his footsteps now trudging along the corridor. 'They are a sound business investment. My bestselling remedies call for their blood and whiskers.'

'How long have you been hiding them, and what

profits have you made since they arrived?' Moore snapped, pursuing Rathder.

'Like I said, my old friend,' Rathder chuckled self-consciously, 'investments take time to—' The wall between the room and the corridor shook suddenly, and the cats froze, hearing Rathder groan. 'Cornelius!' his voice croaked, strangled. 'We are partners, not enemies! There is no need for violence!'

'We're dead if we cannot pay up!' Moore snapped, his anxiety wavering the fury rumbling in his throat. 'Your dulpickle wildcat plot will get us nowhere!' There was another thump as Rathder's body was released from the wall. A swift rustle followed as he scrambled to his feet. 'We need to think of something bigger. A scheme that will take us out of the gutter and change our miserable lives forever! Then we can leave this plague-infested, poverty-festering hellhole and take our riches abroad.'

'Come, come,' Rathder crooned, his footsteps quickening. 'I have something inside that will take our worries away and feed our imaginations.'

Rathder's and Moore's footsteps disappeared into the depths of the apothecary shop, and Beauty trotted to the latched door in the corner of the room with Asta at her heels. Through the cracks in the timber, they could just make out the two men standing on the shop floor lighting long clay pipes and talking to each other through clouds of smoke. Asta pricked her ears, straining to hear their conversation. Ash tentatively joined them, his worry etching deeply across his forehead.

'If we go now while the fair is setting up,' Moore was urging, 'I can get us backstage, and we'll see the animals before anyone else. We'll know which are the fiercest, then we'll place our bets, and fortune will be ours!'

Rathder grinned and his eyes glittered with greed.

CHAPTER TEN

WAR

For the rest of the day, while Beauty and Ash were curled up together on the floor, Asta sat on the windowsill and peered out into the human world. If she was going to escape it, she had to understand it. She was fascinated and frightened by it, yet the longer she watched the more her curiosity appeased her fears.

Plainly dressed people wandered up and down the streets and walked beneath the jettied floors of houses to avoid the rubbish and excrement being thrown from the windows above. Asta's eyes followed women carrying baskets of shopping for their employers in the crooks of their arms. They hiked up their thick skirts to step over the filth while a scattering of men, lugging crates on their shoulders full of wares to trade, cried out to the residents inside their homes, and tempted them to buy *frrreeeesh fish from Essex!* and '*juuuuuicy raspberries from Kent*'. Other more finely dressed people glided past, gazing absentmindedly out of carriages pulled by horses, clip-clopping against the cobbled roads.

As the hours passed, there wasn't a moment of quiet. There was always a church bell chiming in the distance or a person marching from place to place, shouting or guffawing. Asta sighed. The wildcats would never escape unnoticed on the ground. Even if they were to sprint through the streets, a human would be lurking round every corner. Asta stared up at the rooftops, built so close together that they almost touched. Up there, no human roamed. Only plump, contented pigeons waddled across the terracotta tiles. That would be the safest getaway, and her mouth watered, imagining the birds between her jaws.

The sky was turning opal when Rathder and Moore stomped back up the garden path, their faces bright with ideas as they talked rapidly to one another in hushed tones.

Beauty's head darted from where it rested on Ash's flank, her ears pricking at her master's voice. The back door creaked open and closed, and the men muttered excitedly as they hurried down the corridor into the apothecary shop. Beauty bounded to the door and meowed loudly and incessantly until Rathder cracked it ajar.

'Hello, my darling girl,' he gushed as she slipped out.

The door creaked shut behind her.

'Oh, Ash.' Asta leaped from the windowsill to where he lay on the floor and pressed her head against his, her heart skipping at finally being alone with him. 'I've wanted to talk to you for so long.'

Ash purred. 'Why didn't you before?' he asked with a confused smile.

'How could I?' Asta frowned. 'Beauty has not left our side since we arrived.'

'Anything you say to me you can say to her,' Ash replied, perplexed. 'She's our friend.'

Asta shook her head. 'I don't want to be her friend – I don't trust her, and she hates me.'

'Maybe that's because you haven't been nice to her,' Ash retorted. The sting in his voice struck Asta like a blow to the chest. 'After everything she and our master have done to protect us, you should be grateful.'

'*Our master?*' Asta repeated, her hackles rising. 'Do you believe we are better off in this human prison than free in our forest?'

'You *don't?*' He gaped. 'We'd never survive the dangers of the woods. Don't you remember what happened to Mother?' There was a pause, and the wildcats' eyes filled with tears. 'And what about all those animals we saw trapped in those cages this morning? We don't stand a chance against humans. It is safer serving them than risking our lives on our own.'

'We belong in the wild,' Asta corrected, a lump swelling her throat. It hurt her to argue with him. He was all she had left, and the thought of losing him made her ache. 'Beauty is a domestic cat – a human plaything – she knows nothing about freedom. She wants us to stay so her master can steal our blood and whiskers and sell his potions. Then he can make enough money to move to a bigger house and garden. They don't care about us. They are trying to control us so we won't run home.'

'This *is* our home, Asta,' Ash flared.

Asta flinched. His tone was harsher than she had ever known.

Ash sighed, his jaw hardening. 'You aren't as close to Beauty as I am. She cares about me. I know she is protecting us. She understands the humans better than you and I ever will. She believes we can do great things here that we could never have done in the wild.'

'That doesn't mean we are safe, or that she has good intentions for us.'

'Beauty *hasn't* lied!' Ash hissed. Asta's mouth fell open, not recognizing him. 'We've seen what humans are capable of, and this city is crawling with them! They all want to skin us, stuff us, eat us or abuse us. And the forest is no better – the hunters knew we were there, and it was only a matter of time before they found us! We will die if we do not ally ourselves with humans.' Ash heaved a deep, irritated breath. 'We just have to get used to their world. Have faith, Asta. We won't be locked in this room forever. Our master will make enough money and move us to a bigger house with a garden, just like Beauty said.'

'I'd rather live free and die free than be a slave to human want and need.' Asta smouldered, feeling bruised and betrayed by Ash's words.

'There is no freedom when your life is in danger!' Ash scoffed, his eyes narrowing with contempt. 'The only reason we're alive is because Beauty and our master rescued us from starvation in the wild. Even you couldn't hunt without Mother's help. Now we don't have to worry. Most wild animals dream of such a gift . . .'

'You're wrong!' Asta interrupted, a throbbing fury flooding her senses. 'Most wild animals would wilt and die in this place! I will never accept it. And Mother never would have accepted it either!'

She padded to the corner of the room, unable to stop the sobs rising in her throat. She retreated beneath a chair with her back towards her brother, her devastation seizing her limbs. Her hopes of returning to the forest together were fading, and the thought of waiting any longer, imprisoned in the human world, suffocated the air in her lungs. With despair humming through her, she hid her face behind her tail and wept, feeling grateful for the gathering darkness and that the day would soon be over.

The cold, prickling silence of conflict was still radiating around the wildcats when Beauty slipped back into the room beside Rathder's ankles. She hurried to Ash and nuzzled into his neck while Rathder placed two bowls filled with meagre cuts of meat on the ground. He crouched low, his gaze lingering on Ash in the fading light before his grey eyes flitted about the room in search of Asta.

'See you on the morrow, my pretties,' Rathder smiled, spotting Asta under the chair. Her gaze darkened with hatred. Beauty stared up at her master with a soft mew and blinked adoringly at him as he walked out of the room.

'Sleep well.' He affectionately smacked his lips at her and closed the door behind him.

It was the middle of the night when Asta roused sharply, her spine tingling, hearing a monstrous yowl. She glanced about the room. A cat was caterwauling, and a metallic scent was creeping up her nose.

'Asta, how could you!' Ash cried.

Asta frowned, unsure if she was dreaming or of how long she had been sleeping. Bewildered, she looked about her, trying to understand what was happening. It was then that she stared down at her paws and gasped. They were sticky with blood.

Asta turned. Beauty lay collapsed on her side between the wildcat cages. Her face was mauled with scratches, and more wounds across her chest were pooling blackly on to the floorboards.

'Asta was so quiet tonight. I only wanted to check she was all right,' Beauty said meekly, trembling as Ash tenderly licked her cheek. 'She's gone mad,' she whispered to him, her eyes rounding in terror. She howled loudly and persistently. 'I thought she was going to kill me.'

'What?' Asta retorted over the cat's cries, her brow furrowing with confusion. She went to them, her bloody paws tacking against the floor. 'I don't know what she's—'

'You've gone too far, Asta!' Ash snapped, protectively crouching over Beauty and glaring at Asta as she neared. Her ears pulled back. Rathder's hurried footsteps pounded from within. 'Don't come any closer!'

'But, Ash!' Asta protested. 'You have to listen—'

The door flung open and closed. Rathder raced inside the room, holding a brass candlestick. It billowed orange flames and black shadows around his gaunt face and ghoulishly hollowed his cheeks and eyes. He groaned in horror, seeing his beloved Beauty writhing and whining in pain on the ground.

'Evil creature!' Rathder roared as his grey eyes found Asta and her bloody paws. He slammed the candlestick upon the sideboard, and Asta bolted back under the chair that she had been sleeping peacefully beneath only a few minutes before. 'I'll get you for this!' Rathder hurled a book at her, forcing Asta to retreat further into the room. 'My darling girl,' he cooed, swiftly turning out of the room with Ash trotting at his heels. 'My poor, precious girl.'

The door slammed shut, leaving Asta alone in the dark.

CHAPTER ELEVEN

THE FAIR

The following afternoon, Rathder stormed into the room armed with a broom that he held across his chest as though it was an axe. Moore burst in beside him, tightly gripping a large sheet of chainmail in his fists. Malice oozed from the men as they stomped about the floor, and their jaws hardened as they scowled and dipped their heads below the tables and chairs in search of Asta.

From behind a thick table leg in the corner of the room, Asta pressed her body against the wall. Her green eyes hunted for an escape, but there was no way out. She had never seen the windows open, and the metal lattice surround was impossible to break through. Her only chance was to hide and then sprint through the door when the men gave up their hunt for her and returned to the apothecary shop.

'Where is the wretch?' Rathder growled, throwing a

chair on its side in frustration. Asta tensed as the timber smacked against the ground.

'Are you sure she's still in here?' Moore muttered, ducking his head under the sideboard where Asta was hiding. Asta froze behind its thick timber leg, not daring to blink as his dark eyes scoured the space between them. Her heart pounded so loudly behind her ribs that she feared it would give her away. She bared her claws, her fur stiffening as she readied herself to pounce. But a moment later Moore stood upright and stomped away. Asta heaved a sigh of relief.

'Nonsense!' Rathder retorted. 'Nothing has come in or out of here since last night!'

'Well, she ain't in here!' Moore snapped back. 'We've looked everywhere!'

Asta flattened herself against the floor, edged towards the door and prayed to go unnoticed as she stared at the men's leather boots, shuffling uncertainly nearby.

'Pah! You've lost her, you old fossil.' Moore sighed impatiently, setting off towards the door. Its latch clunked open and slowly cracked ajar. Asta nudged forward, her blood thumping. She held her breath, willing the men to pass through it.

'Rubbish!' Rathder scoffed, abruptly bending beneath the sideboard.

Asta gasped as her bright green eyes met his cold, grey glare.

His face contorted into a grimace. 'There she is!'

Panic thrummed through Asta as Rathder shoved the broom beneath the table and swung it violently from side to side, battering Asta hard against the face and then the flank. She bolted from her hiding place and dashed for the other side of the room. But Rathder was fast. Hurtling towards her, he smashed the broom against her spine with an almighty thwack, and Asta yowled in pain as its timber rod pinned her to the floor.

'Snatch that fiend!' Rathder screeched.

Moore threw himself upon Asta, the heavy sheet of chainmail in his grasp closing around her before she could catch her breath. She writhed and snarled and hissed beneath it, but it was hopeless. The chainmail was heavy and impenetrable, and her flesh throbbed as her claws and teeth snagged on its metal rings. Moore was swift and strong. In seconds, Asta was scooped into the air and sealed inside a tightly bound sack of steel.

'Good riddance to you,' Rathder sneered through gritted teeth, his head bending towards her as she struggled helplessly. She spat, and a malevolent chuckle rose to Rathder's lips, 'Bring us fortune,' he hissed, his eyes narrowing, 'and may you get what you deserve.'

Smirking, Moore turned out of the room and marched down the gloomy corridor, leading to the back door. It thumped shut behind him, and he strode along Rathder's narrow garden path with Asta swinging from his fist.

She thrashed inside the chainmail sack, her senses tingling with the fresh air that she had not breathed or felt brush against her fur for too many weeks.

She inhaled deeply, memorizing the mix of lavender and rosemary scents so she could find her way back to Ash, and her gaze roved about, taking in the back of Rathder's building, which was rapidly growing smaller in the distance with each of Moore's broad strides. She searched for Ash in every window.

Just as Moore rounded Rathder's low garden wall, she spied her brother silhouetted on an upper windowsill. He watched her, his face and front paws pressed against the glass, but a moment later Beauty dotingly rubbed her head against his and pushed his gaze elsewhere.

Asta growled, knowing Beauty was controlling him under the guise of affection and, as Moore plodded to Fetter Lane, her eyes strained for a last glimpse of her brother.

Moore's boots briskly pounded the ground as he walked through the balmy afternoon sunshine and stepped over the muck and grime strewn across the narrow back streets of the City of London. His breath puffed from his lips, and the musky scent of his sweat rose as he cut across Shoe Lane and headed right along Plumtree Court towards Farringdon Street, where clopping hooves and grinding carriage wheels swallowed his heavy footsteps all the way to West Smithfield.

It was not long before the street became crowded with stalls, tents, platforms and stages, many of which had men hammering nails into timber frames draped in colourful fabrics. Moore slowed to weave through crowds gathering around posters pinned from tall poles that stretched up from all over the street, depicting the first promises of the next two weeks to come at the Bartholomew Fair.

Magicians, bearded women, sword swallowers and jugglers stared out from the paper, and Asta's chest tightened as she saw a long line of pictures of bulls and bears brawling with a circling pack of dogs, nipping and snarling at their ankles.

The posters led Moore to the largest tent where a group of children huddled at a closed double wrought-iron gate. A broad, bright banner, illustrating a vibrant scene of the most popular attraction at the fair, hung above it. In the background, monkeys danced on a high tightrope raised over acrobats somersaulting through the air above men breathing plumes of orange flames. Beside them, beautiful women rode horses cantering around a ring.

The children were muttering excitedly as they wobbled on their tiptoes and pushed their noses through the gaps in the gate. Some lifted their shorter or younger companions in hopes of setting eyes on the performers, whose daring feats were famous for making London's hearts leap and tongues wag. Yet, despite the children's thrill, they uttered disappointed sighs and whispers as the main tent and its heavy drapes remained firmly drawn.

'Move, vile urchins,' Moore growled, pushing the children roughly aside.

A cacophony of protest roared around him. Asta quailed inside the chainmail sack and stared at the children through the gaps in the mesh. She had never seen or heard a group of children before. They were the noisiest creatures she had ever encountered.

'Are you a performer?' a young boy asked. Moore barged past his friends and opened the gate. The children surged around it as he closed it behind him and ignored their barrage of questions.

'Give us a peek, mister!'

'Oh please, mister,' a girl pleaded, snatching at Moore's coat sleeve and tugging it, 'can't you give us—'

'BEGONE, LITTLE TIKES!' Moore whirled on them, his eyebrows knitting into a hair-raising scowl.

The children squealed with fright and hurried away like a shoal of little fish.

*

The children's shrieks faded as Moore shoved aside the heavy drapes and stepped into the main tent, its white canvas casting the late afternoon sunlight into shade. Moore trod across an empty, circular arena with freshly scattered sawdust on the ground. Surrounding the auditorium were tiers of elevated seats that were raised and separated from the floor by a tall timber wall. Four entrances were placed at each quarter of the ring. Moore plodded from one in a straight line towards another, where two men were hammering the last planks of wood round a gated opening leading backstage. The men glanced up from their work for a moment and nodded in recognition. Moore returned the gesture as he reached the gate and slid it open.

Instantly, the scent of many different animals rushed up Asta's nose. The same caged cockerels, rats and badgers she had watched pass Rathder's back window were lined up in a row beside the biggest enclosure, where the mother bear and her cub sat and watched Moore enter and approach another man, scribbling on papers strewn across a table. Behind him, two bulls that Asta also remembered from that morning bellowed from inside a twin-stalled stable.

'Osborne,' Moore uttered gruffly. The grizzled man turned to him, his gaze darting to the chainmail sack in Moore's fist. 'I have a proposition for you.'

Osborne motioned for Moore to join him at the table. Asta was lifted upon it, and she hunched low inside the sack, her green eyes flitting fearfully between the men peering coldly at her. She hissed.

'A tabby?' Osborne scoffed. 'It won't last a second in my baiting ring.'

'This ain't no tabby,' Moore rejoined. 'This is a forest tiger. A wild, *ferocious* beast.'

Osborne edged closer, his icy blue eyes inspecting her bushy tail through the metal mesh. He grunted, seeing Moore was right. 'A small one.'

'Don't judge her too soon,' Moore added. 'You should've seen the mauling she gave Rathder's cat.' There was a pause as Osborne considered this for a moment. 'And it's no bad thing if her size misleads the spectators. If you set the odds right, the better the takings for us both.'

'You forget something.' Osborne stood tall, crossing his arms. 'We don't know how vicious she is in a brawl against another animal. My audience wants blood, not a fleeing, hissing feline. If she fights and loses, the odds will not go in our favour, and she will bring loss, not wealth.'

'There's only one way to find out,' Moore said, searching around him and dragging Asta roughly from the table. She yowled, dangling from his fist once more.

A thin bamboo cane Osborne used to whip the animals was propped up against the table. Moore snatched it and strode towards a small empty cage, lying on the floor on its side. Tucking the bamboo cane under his arm, he grabbed the cage in his spare hand. Slamming it upright beside the bears' enclosure, he shoved Asta through the door and swiftly sealed her inside. The mother bear drew her cub close to her at once and retreated into their pen. Asta backed into her cage, trying to put as much distance between her and the men.

'Let's see what you're made of.' Moore glared at Asta through the bars. Her pupils dilated, a fresh wave of fright and rage rising from the pit of her stomach. Moore stared back at her and glowed with pleasure.

He stabbed the bamboo cane through the bars. Asta snarled and slashed at it furiously, desperate to stop it from jabbing into her. Osborne's and Moore's faces shone with glee. Delighting in her suffering, Moore laughed and thrust the cane into her ribs, harder and harder, until Asta pounced on the stick with a yowl and wrestled with it in a frenzy of teeth and claws.

'Swift, vicious and potentially valuable creature.' Osborne slapped Moore's back. 'She'll do well. But if she does *very* well she could be one of my star attractions this year.' Moore met Osborne's words with a determined smile. 'We'll find out when the fights commence tomorrow.'

Osborne stepped away and returned to his papers, leaving Moore and Asta glowering at one another through the bars of Asta's small cage

'Good girl,' Moore sneered, poking the cane towards Asta once more. She spat venomously and swatted it away, her fur bristling all over her body. Moore chuckled. 'Your spite will bring us riches.'

Asta glared bitterly at him as he retracted the stick and cast it aside. He walked away and disappeared through the open gate, leading back to the arena and the city beyond.

CHAPTER TWELVE

TILIA AND LIPA

At sunset, the humans poked rancid meat and fish through the animal's cages with sticks and left the main tent for the night. As they closed the iron gates with a clink of fastening locks, silence unfurled around the animals. Listening to the men's footsteps fade into the distance, Asta wondered what the next day would bring.

Then Asta's fur stiffened, feeling eyes upon her. Rounding on herself, she came face to face with the bear cub, sitting at the edge of the enclosure that he shared with his mother, which was beside Asta's cage. The cub stared wistfully at a slimy, rotting fish that lolled over the top corner of Asta's pen. It had remained there, untouched, since the humans had tossed it to her. Asta couldn't bring herself to eat it. Even if it had been fresh, she could not have stomached it for the worry writhing in her gut.

Standing on her hind legs, Asta dabbed her paws through the ceiling of her cage. With a final glance at the bear club, she aimed and propelled the fish towards him. It smacked against his enclosure, and the bear cub's face brightened as he inched towards it and reached his paw through the bars. The tip of his pink tongue popped out of the corner of his mouth in concentration as he dragged the fish to him and retrieved it in his teeth. He scurried past his mother staring dolefully at the floor of their enclosure, and ate it noisily. The mother bear turned to him. She frowned in puzzlement, searching their pen. Her gaze soon found Asta, hunched low and watching her warily from the neighbouring cage. The bear's expression softened at once, realizing the wildcat was responsible for the extra food.

'Thank you,' the mother bear said softly, padding away from the cub to sit on her haunches opposite Asta. 'I'm Tilia. This is my son, Lipa.'

'I'm Asta,' Asta replied, ears pricking with friendliness as she watched the mother bear, who looked sadly over her shoulder at her son, still wolfing down the food. Tilia's claws had been clipped, and Asta could tell by

the way the bear's fur hung
from her broad
frame that she
should have
more flesh on
her bones.

Yet, despite this, Asta's
instincts warned her that Tilia's strong jaw
and determined, dark eyes meant that she was still a
formidable creature.

'He's always hungry,' Tilia sighed. 'If we were in the
wild, he would be foraging on his own soon. Osborne and

his men never give us enough to eat.'

'I was taken from the wild too.' Asta's heart stirred, feeling an immediate kinship with the bear. 'How long have you been here?'

'Too long,' the bear said. 'I was snared in the Carpathian Mountains while Lipa and his sister were still growing inside me. I was pitted against packs of dogs straight away. Their hunger for combat matched the blood lust of the men, who came in packs and gambled on the outcome.

'After I gave birth, I worried for my cubs. I attacked any human that dared to come near us, and for a time the humans let us be. I ceased fighting, and they fed me more so I could nurse my young. Those weeks are some of the most precious memories I have. But it was short-lived. The day after my daughter refused my milk, the men plucked her from me and sold her.' Tilia bowed her head. 'She died soon after we were separated. That's why they have kept Lipa close to me.' She looked at him, her eyes clouding with despair. She lowered her voice to a whisper. 'I wish I could get him away from here. I know they will take him from me soon.' Her dark brown eyes glistened as they flicked to him, obliviously eating the fish. 'He will suffer the same fate as us, or worse.'

'Is there really no escape?' Asta asked, her gaze travelling over the other caged animals, anxiously nibbling their fleas or, like Asta, ignoring their food.

The bear shook her head. 'It's rare. No teeth or claws can break the metal on our cages, and when we are released the humans miss nothing. Their eyes and ears are sharp whenever their money exchanges hands, and their dogs' noses are keen. In the past, those that have managed to escape are either caught in the act or swiftly recaptured, and sometimes killed, especially when the brawls are in towns or cities where we are surrounded and outnumbered by humans.'

'Tell me what happens in the brawls,' Asta said timidly. Tilia's mahogany eyes darkened. 'I need to know.'

The bear glanced protectively at her cub and lowered her voice further. Asta inched forward and pricked her ears high up on her head to hear Tilia's whispers.

'The small animals go into the arena first,' Tilia began. 'First, the rats are set loose in the ring, and they are chased by terriers who rattle the life from them. Then the cockerels battle one another, some of them dressed with decorative spurs on their legs to cause the most havoc. The dog fights are next,' Tilia sighed, 'and after that the baiting begins.'

'Baiting?' Asta asked, her hackles rising.

'The humans chain animals and harass them with

dogs for sport.' Asta's ears flattened as Tilia went on. 'The badgers start. Dogs are set upon them inside boxes and a clock times how fast they can drag the poor creatures into the ring. Those that can do so within a minute win the humans the most money. The bulls and bears face the dogs for the grand finale. We are chained to a stake that is impaled in the ground. Then the dogs torment us. The more we hurl them into the air, the more the audience cheers.'

'What will happen to me?' Asta swallowed. Tilia was silent, her brow furrowed with reluctance. 'Please,' Asta added, 'I need to know.'

Tilia paused to look Asta up and down. 'I've seen a wildcat fight once. It was baited after the badgers. That collar round your neck will be chained to the stake in the centre of the arena. Then the humans will set dogs on you from all sides of the ring, just like me and the bulls. They say fighting the bulls tenderizes the meat.'

Asta shivered and swallowed hard, trying to quiet the terror scuttling through her.

Tilia's brow furrowed with sympathy. 'You must use your wits and show no mercy, for they will give you none. Their dogs – old English bulldogs and mastiffs – have been bred to fight since puppyhood. The better you brawl, the more valuable you will become, and Osborne will preserve your life and turn you into an attraction.'

'But I don't know how to fight.' Asta shuddered, her voice cracking. 'I can't even hunt rabbit on my own. I've never fought anything before. Only my brother, but that was just playing.'

'That will change,' Tilia said softly. 'Everyone fights when their life is in danger.'

Asta's gaze travelled to the other animals and wondered which were meek and which were bold, and who would crumple and who would triumph in the ring.

'What if we refuse to fight?' Hope tumbled out of Asta's mouth. 'We'll be worthless to the men! They'll tire of us and free us from the brawls!'

'That's certain death.' Tilia shook her head. 'Those that resist combat have their necks wrung or are torn to pieces in the ring.'

'But if we're killed –' Asta frowned – 'they won't have any animals for the fights. It's in their interest to keep us alive.'

'I wish that were true, but there is no stopping it, Asta,' Tilia added sadly. 'Men, like the man that brought you here, sell animals to Osborne every day. He is never in short supply because he is famous for earning a fortune, and he pays handsomely for the right stock. New animals arrive every morning to replace those that have perished in combat the previous day.'

'Even you?'

'Even me.' Tilia nodded slowly, her brow creasing with defeat. 'You are right. Bears are rarer, and that makes us more valuable, but a man like Osborne is unpredictable. He is driven by wealth and, if a bear loses its fighting spirit and stops drawing the crowds, he can rig a baiting match and profit from a bear's death.'

'Why do the humans want to see us suffer?' Asta's lips trembled. 'What pleasure can they take in hurting animals?'

'Because they are predators, and it excites them,' Tilia growled. 'But they devour their prey unlike any other animal we know in the wild, and they are almost unbeatable. Although their flesh is weak, their minds are more cunning than ours, and there's little we can do to outwit their tricks and inventions. They believe animals serve human beings, yet their hunger for blood will never match their lust for gold.

'Every human has ambitions for riches,' Tilia continued, 'and the Bartholomew Fair is a feeding ground. Men like Osborne delight further in our suffering because the more blood and death during the fights, the greedier the gambling becomes. The brawls also bring crowds of paying customers. As our fights reach a climax, the spectators whir into a fever of excitement. Their cries and cheers entice more people to the arena, at exactly the same time, as the fair's main event is about to begin. Then, once the baiting comes to an end, a crush of people buy tickets in a frenzy of anticipation for the acrobats, whose daring stunts draw gasps from the crowds until the fair is closed for the night. The same routine plays out day after day, night after night, until the fair is over. We are a cog in the machine, Asta, and our survival rests on our will to live.'

Asta listened with outrage bubbling inside her. She narrowed her eyes and vowed not to let the humans break her spirit. She would fight for Ash, and somehow, she would find her way back to him and persuade him to leave Beauty and the evils of the human world.

At that moment, a roar of voices blustered outside. All the animals shuffled nervously in their cages with their ears flattening at the noise. Lipa scurried to Tilia, who drew him close.

'What's that?' Asta whispered, her heart thudding against her ribs.

'It's the opening ceremony of the fair,' Tilia said gravely. 'Tomorrow, it will begin.'

CHAPTER THIRTEEN

THE RING

Asta woke with a start, hearing men shout irritably as they rushed back and forth past the caged animals in a last frenetic attempt to organize the main tent for the crowds they expected to arrive in the coming hours. Asta backed into her pen, her eyes flicking anxiously between the humans.

The night had been hard on Asta. Tilia and Lipa had encouraged her to sleep to save her strength for the following day, but whenever Asta closed her eyes her mind had twisted with slavering dogs pursuing her round the baiting ring. Asta passed the hours fitfully burrowing and gnawing at the metal of her cage to the sounds of the other restless animals, trapped and whimpering under the same cloud of dread.

The tent was brightening when she finally gave up and

allowed her eyes to close. She roused soon afterwards, scenting the smell of fear. An eerie quietness had descended over the animals as they hunched low in their cages and contemplated the brawls to come. She looked at Tilia and Lipa, tightly curled up together in the furthest corner of their enclosure, with their backs turned to any prying eyes. Asta sighed sadly and stared at the grubby floor of her cage.

She had never felt so alone.

The sun climbed the clear morning sky and shone upon the hum of chattering crowds, drummers and trumpeters that swelled into a hubbub of festivity as the first day of the Bartholomew Fair got underway. By noon, the smells of unwashed bodies, roasting meat and tobacco smoke wafted into the arena as a crush of people took their seats in readiness for the animal brawls to begin.

Osborne swung a silver-topped cane by his side and paced regally before the animals' cages. He was dressed in a long, fine coat, stockings, leather shoes and a periwig. Asta glared coldly at him from behind the bars of her pen. Tilia protectively pushed Lipa behind her and glowered at him from the neighbouring enclosure.

'My creatures —' a self-satisfied smile drew across

Osborne's thin lips as he fingered the top of his cane – 'now it is time to test your mettle.'

Pivoting grandly on his heel, he strode into the arena to the sounds of cheering applause before the crowd hushed to hear him announce the start of the baiting matches. A moment later, the humans roared with anticipation and the animals quailed, knowing they would soon be fighting for their lives.

Just as Tilia had predicted, the rats were the first to be taken into the ring, and they squirmed and squeaked inside their cages as stone-faced men took them away.

The noise from the arena was terrifying. The humans hollered, whooped and yelled over the sounds of dogs growling, yapping, barking and yelping. As soon as the commotion blared in a crescendo of fury and delight, Asta knew the match was over, and the next round of brawls would soon begin. By the time the badgers were taken into the ring, the smaller coops backstage were empty of rats, and only one cockerel remained alive, clucking softly to himself in a haze of horror and exhaustion. The next clamour of blood lust marked the end of another tussle, and Asta's heart began to pound, feeling every human hoot and cry crawl over her fur.

'I'm scared, Tilia,' Asta whispered to the mother

bear, who was cradling Lipa in her arms.

'Remember to use the guile that nature has given you, Asta,' Tilia said firmly as two men swiftly marched to Asta's cage. Asta backed into it as far as she could manage and hissed at them. 'Keep hold of the will to live and you *will* survive,' Tilia added urgently.

The men draped chainmail over the door to Asta's cage, and with a sudden tip and an almighty shove she was hurled from her enclosure into the metal mesh. The men pinned her to the ground with swift, confident hands. Kneeling on her, they briefly lifted the chainmail and clipped a long chain to the steel collar round her neck. Seconds later, she was caught up inside a steel sack and swinging from a man's grasp.

The men stomped into the arena. A wave of noise and a heady surge of scents of sweat and blood struck Asta in the face. She shuddered, staring through the gaps in the chainmail. Hundreds of people with rosy, perspiring faces peered down at her from tiers of benches surrounding the fighting area. Men and women from across society – gentlemen, civil servants, dandies, apprentices, butchers, maids and bakers – chattered to one another in a writhing den of vice and greed. Many shouted jovially between sips from tankards filled with ale, and spittle spewed from their lips as they laughed and sang, while couples canoodled alongside other young men and women, glancing through the auditorium and preening themselves in the hope of catching the sights of admirers.

It was then that Asta's sharp eyes caught a flash of black swooping over their heads, and a large raven fluttered to a pole overlooking the audience. It fixed its gaze on Asta.

'NEXT, FOR YOUR VIEWING PLEASURE . . .' Osborne cried with his arms grandiosely stretched above his head.

An excited hush descended on the audience. They edged forward on their seats and eagerly watched the man carrying Asta in the chainmail sack. He carried her to the centre of the fighting ring where a short metal rod protruded from the dirt and blood-stained sawdust. Once again, two men pressed Asta to the ground, lifted the chainmail and clipped the chain attached to her collar to a small hoop welded to the stake.

'Worshipped by the early Celts of Scotland and still used as a symbolic crest by some of the Scottish clans,' Osborne crowed, 'I give you, the FOR-EST TIG-ER!'

The chainmail was whipped away from Asta's body, and Osborne and the two men dashed away from her, leaving her cowering beside the rod in the centre of the ring with her eyes flitting anxiously around the blur of humans circling her.

'Do not be mistaken,' Osborne chuckled, noting some of the confused expressions in the audience, 'this is not a tabby cat! Observe its muscular frame, its broad head and bushy tail – this is a ferocious beast capable of disembowelling its victims in fatal conflicts. A wildcat is timid until it is cornered. When provoked into action, its skills in combat have been compared to a small tiger, unleashing itself upon its prey like a fiend straight from hell!'

The crowd murmured excitedly and Osborne's bookmakers, each wearing a wide-brimmed black hat trimmed with an ostrich feather, started weaving through the audience to collect the first bets.

'The wildcat has ambushed shepherds and mauled their dogs to death before slashing the throats of the men themselves,' Osborne added. He paused for dramatic effect, and more people in the audience waved to the bookmakers. 'What say you? How will this forest tiger fare against two of my brawniest dogs?'

On cue, two men entered from opposite entrances into the arena. Each had a broad, stocky dog tugging from a chain held taut at their hips. The largest was a mastiff, whose enormous piebald frame and a massive head with a mask of black fur looked more like a bear than any dog Asta had seen before. The other was an old English bulldog with a smattering of brown patches marking its white muscular body. Asta ached with terror, her gaze roving between their fierce features, leering eyes and grins, slobbering with bloodthirstiness.

'Place your wagers!' Osborne crowed. 'Then the baiting will commence!'

Excitement radiated across the audience as men and women cried out and hungrily shook their purses of coins in the air to attract the attention of Osborne's bookmakers rushing through the auditorium to meet demand.

Asta scratched at her collar with her paws and thrashed her head from side to side. If only she could break it, then she would be free of the chain. She could easily scale the timber wall that separated the raised tiers of benches from the fighting ring. She stared at the crowds of people and searched for the easiest route out of the tent, and she shivered, knowing the only way to escape would be to sprint through the throng. She frantically shook her head and choked herself against the shackle round her neck. She yowled. It was hopeless; the steel band was bolted and impossible to remove.

It was then that she spied Rathder and Moore, glaring down at her, unblinking and muttering to one another with hard, determined jaws. She froze, her mind flooding with thoughts of Ash. No matter what happened in the coming minutes, she had to find her way back to him.

'FINAL BETS!' Osborne called, raising his silver-topped cane higher into the air. A flurry of activity ensued before he slammed it back into the ground, signalling the end of the gambling.

The mastiff and the old English bulldog's ears pricked, recognizing the sound. They whimpered eagerly as their handlers straddled their backs like horses and clutched their cheeks in their fists. Asta's blood thundered through her veins, watching the dogs thrust forward. But the men held them fast, and with each lurch the dogs jerked painfully in the men's grasps, encouraging a furious savageness, and the dog's growls grew fiercer with every frustrated movement.

'May the baiting BE-GIN!' Osborne declared.

The crowd roared. The men gave the mastiff and the old English bulldog a final shove and hurried away.

The dogs barrelled towards Asta, who was trembling all over with terror. She tried to anticipate which dog would reach her first. She lowered her stance, readying herself to pounce, her fur bristling and her green eyes flicking between the fast-approaching hounds.

The bulldog leaped, and a shriek of awe went up through the crowd as Asta jumped clear and landed safely on her paws a few feet away. The mastiff plunged towards her, and Asta sprung upwards, swiping with her paws, and the dog howled in pain as the wildcat's claws raked its muzzle. The bulldog rounded on them with a snarl. But Asta reacted quickly and, with a swift twist in the air, she narrowly missed its open jaws and vaulted from its back to a rambunctious round of applause.

Asta sprinted away from the dogs, now bounding after her and snapping at her heels. In a matter of seconds, the chain tugged taut, strangling her by the collar. A collective gasp swept over the auditorium, yet Asta harnessed the abrupt halt, dodging the mastiff and the bulldog hurtling past her to veer in a different direction.

The dogs surged at the wildcat again. But Asta was fast and averted their blundering attacks with a slash of her claws and sprang out of harm's way, again and again. Only once did the bulldog catch her by the leg. It ground its teeth on her bone with a swift thrash of his head and slammed her on to the ground. Asta's instincts shot into action. Instantly whirling on him, she stabbed her fangs into its chest and raked her claws across its underbelly. The bulldog yelped and released its grip, and Asta sped away, leaving the bulldog to stumble and collapse on its side. Blood pooled beneath him, and the Mastiff halted, its hackles stiffening as it drooled and snarled at the wildcat. Confidence thrummed through Asta, realizing her advantage. The dogs battled with their teeth alone, yet she had her claws as well. The mastiff and the wildcat glowered at one another, their eyes narrowing and their lips pulling back round their fangs.

With a fearsome cry, Asta and the mastiff charged, and the audience drew a breath, watching the distance close between them. Feeling time slow, Asta stared, waiting for the mastiff's slow and deliberate legs to bend and jump, then in an eye blink she leaped to the left and rocketed upwards. A second later, her paws landed on the mastiff's spine and, piercing her teeth into the back of its neck, she brought its huge, lumbering body crashing to the ground.

A tumult of elation went up through the auditorium. Men and women whooped and clapped their hands, delighted by the ferocity and quick-wittedness of the wildcat that had filled their purses and brought spectacle to their afternoon. Within the throng, Rathder and Moore jumped up and down for joy. By forfeiting Asta to the baiting ring like Moore had insisted, Rathder had risked losing half of his live wildcat investment, but now Asta had proved her worth. Both men hooted heartily and dared to believe that one day their debts would be repaid.

The dogs were dragged out while Asta's collar was yanked into the centre of the arena. A young man was pulling her chain through the hoop welded to the end of the baiting stake, and she struggled as it rapidly shortened.

As soon as she felt the metal rod against her fur, another man dashed to her, flinging the length of chainmail over her. In moments, the man had pinned her to the ground and unfastened her chain and she was scooped into the steel sack again, with the clamour of humans and the jingle of their coins ringing in her ears.

Asta panted. The terror, exhaustion and the relief that she was still alive tumbled through her limbs, and before she could catch her breath she collapsed into a black and heady faint.

CHAPTER FOURTEEN

ISAAC, COSIMA AND ROSIE

The cheering of delighted people soon became as normal to Asta as the wind rustling through the trees in the forest. Day after day, she fought for her life, chained to the baiting stake. Each afternoon, once the rats, cockerel, dogs and badger-baiting had ceased, Asta took her turn, facing the crowds, and brawled against Osborne's hounds under the watchful gaze of Rathder and Moore, and the raven perched high above the throng.

The terror Asta felt in the ring never left her, but she harnessed it, realizing it kept her alive. The crowds had never encountered such a swift and ferocious creature and, while at first she faced only two dogs, Osborne soon forced three and four upon her. Yet still she survived, and Osborne, Rathder and Moore grinned with glee as they lined their pockets with every victory.

Asta was growing up fast in the baiting ring, and although it terrified her it was making her fiercer, and her hopes for the wild strengthened. When she returned to the forest with Ash, she could teach him what she had learned. They would not go hungry, nor would they be under threat from any hunter that came near them again. Whether he cared or not, Ash was always with Asta. Her thoughts often drifted to him, and she often wondered whether he had become a fat and lazy domestic cat, preened and fawned over by Beauty. Asta's hackles rose, seeing the British blue's smug, smiling face flash in her mind. Every sinew in her body flared, knowing Beauty had used Ash's grief and vulnerability to weave a tangle of anxiety in his mind. The brother she knew was wild and curious; he was used to scaling trees and bounding after her through bracken. But now he was imprisoned and isolated inside Rathder's house.

Each evening, the baiting matches came to a close with Tilia returning to her and Lipa's enclosure, and the tightness in Asta's chest would always ease. She found great comfort in the mother bear, who nurtured and mentored Asta before and after every brawl. Even when she was bloody and exhausted, Tilia had wise words to share. The three of them would rest together and slumber through the final hours of each day, through the hubbub and festivity of the acrobatic performances that brought the fair to a riotous end.

In the darkest hours of the first night of the fair when the auditoriums were empty of spectators, and Osborne and his men were celebrating his triumphs in the bawdiest taverns in London, two acrobats, dressed in their fine costumes under dark hooded cloaks, crept lightly into the backstage baiting area, and hurriedly slipped hard-boiled eggs stuffed with herbs through the bars of the animals' cages. Asta flinched, feeling the smooth, white oval roll and brush against her fur, and she hissed when she saw a capuchin monkey staring into her cage from the man's shoulder. Its black tail was hooked about his neck, and its little pink face and dark eyes flitted around the tent from inside a flash of white fur coating its head and shoulders.

'It's all right,' the monkey hushed, leaping to the top of Asta's cage from the man's shoulder as he stepped away towards Tilia and Lipa. 'You have nothing to fear. I'm Rosie and this is Isaac and Cosima. These eggs will keep you strong. Our friend Miriam made them with plant remedies, especially for you.'

'I don't trust anything human,' Asta growled, turning her back on Rosie and the food. 'Leave me alone.'

'Not all humans are bad,' Rosie replied softly. 'Cosima and Isaac rescued me when I fled from a cruel master who beat me until I was almost dead. Miriam is the same. They all hate the baiting matches. They want to help animals, not hurt them. I promise you.'

'Look, my love, a mother and her cub,' Isaac sighed sadly.

Cosima's eyes misted with worry when she saw Tilia. 'They look like the woodcut that your aunt has hanging in her kitchen.' Her Italian accent was lyrical and warm compared to Isaac's English tones.

'Yes, it's of Blind Bess and her cub.' Isaac regarded Tilia and Lipa, his brow creasing with difficult memories. 'My uncle was shot trying to free them from men like Osborne. My aunt has never forgiven herself for failing to release them the night before like they had planned. My uncle and the bears would be alive if they had succeeded. She still grieves for him.' The couple regarded one another gravely and exchanged many words in silence. 'Come.' He squeezed Cosima's hand. 'Let's go.'

'Rosie, come,' Cosima whispered, softly clicking her tongue. The monkey's little head looked for the sound at once. 'Osborne and his men will flay us if they catch us here.'

'Eat up. The eggs will do you good,' Rosie whispered. 'We'll be back.'

She briskly jumped to the ground and sprang up Cosima's long sleeve to the back of her neck. Cosima lifted her hood over the monkey and, grasping Isaac's outstretched hand, the acrobats skittered out of the tent with a cat-like grace.

Asta, Tilia and Lipa gobbled the eggs and felt their sustenance; their flavour was flowery, rich and wild. The eggs calmed their nerves, and the three of them slept more soundly than they had since they could remember.

Cosima, Isaac and Rosie had come every night after that, but they weren't the only visitors backstage. From the second morning, Osborne started parading people in front of the animals before the baiting matches. Instantly, Tilia dragged Lipa into the depths of their enclosure, drew him into her chest and turned their backs to the men. Asta growled, spying the same long bamboo cane with which Moore had tormented her within Osborne's grasp.

'The Carpathian Mountain bear,' Osborne began, pacing grandiosely and clattering the end of the bamboo cane across the bars of Tilia and Lipa's cell. A finely dressed gentleman and his servant followed his steps with two gruff men wearing brown caps, who stood listening to Osborne's speech with their arms crossed and their cold eyes travelling across the animal cages. 'These fearsome beasts roam

Europe's loftiest peaks, darkest woods and savage lands and are unmoved by the packs of wolves and vicious lynxes, prowling through the same trees and mountain ranges searching for prey.'

'Hmmm, never seen a "fearsome beast" that's so shy,' one of the gruff capped men said under his breath, and his friend sniggered in reply.

Osborne's nostrils flared. 'Behold, a mother bear protecting its cub!' he rejoined. Swivelling swiftly on his heel, he poked the bamboo cane through the bars of the bear's cage and jabbed it into Tilia's back. A fierce snarl rose in Asta's throat, watching the bear hunch tighter round Lipa. But the more Tilia resisted, the harder Osborne struck, and a few moments later Tilia swatted the stick away with an almighty roar that made the men stumble backwards in alarm. Osborne smiled with satisfaction as Tilia unwittingly revealed a glimpse of Lipa to their prying eyes.

'How old is the cub?' the finely dressed gentleman asked, tentatively stepping forward.

'Eighteen months, give or take,' Osborne replied, 'and with the rugged Carpathian Mountains coursing through his veins he'll grow to be a fine fighter.'

Tilia drew Lipa into her breast.

'Oh no, no, no. I don't want him to fight.' The gentleman shook his head, his eyes twinkling with fancy. 'I want him to be a dancer. He'd be a fine addition to my menagerie. My guests would marvel, and my parties would be notorious.'

'That's a baiting bear if ever I saw one,' the tallest gruff man scoffed in disagreement. 'He'd be wasted, prancing around for the upper classes. This animal could grow to be the champion of the Bear Garden on Bankside and as famous as Sackerson – or Blind Bess before she was shot by the Puritan pleasure thieves—'

'When you see his mother brawl against my hounds,' Osborne interrupted, ushering the men out of the tent with the wry smile, knowing hooked customers when he saw them, 'you can put your arguments to rest. In the meantime, my bear cub has many more viewings before the day is up, and I must not keep any of them waiting.'

The men strode from the tent, muttering their ambitions to their companions. They crowded Osborne, asking him questions and offering prices, but Osborne was a shrewd businessman. He answered succinctly, for the briefer he spoke, the more the men would fear losing something they wanted, and then they would part with a tidier sum.

Lipa nestled into Tilia's belly fur, and the mother stifled a sob.

Asta's chest tugged. There had to be something she could do. But days passed and still Asta and Tilia could think of nothing.

Three nights after the men first viewed Lipa, Cosima, Isaac and Rosie slipped into the shadows and delivered Miriam's herbal eggs as usual. Relief thrummed through Asta, seeing them approach. Tilia and Lipa had remained entwined throughout the day and had barely uttered a word. The wildcat and the mother bear had been more ferocious than ever in the baiting ring. Both animals found the brawling a release for their desperation and fury. But as soon as Asta was returned to her cage, her mind had continued whirring anxiously, knowing time was running out before the bears would be torn apart forever.

'You are looking brighter already,' Cosima's musical voice whispered as she swiftly pushed two eggs into Asta's cage. 'Miriam says the stars are favouring you. Keep going, *gattina*. We'll keep you strong and that will keep you safe.'

Cosima turned to the bears' enclosure and Asta mewed to Rosie perched on her shoulder.

'Rosie,' Asta said urgently. Rosie hopped from Cosima's shoulder. She leaped upon Asta's cage and her curious little eyes gleamed as they met Asta's in the shadows. 'We need your help. There has to be a way for Tilia, Lipa and me to get out of here.'

'No one has ever escaped and survived.' Rosie shook her head. 'The main tent is accessed by gates alone and it is locked at night and surrounded by high walls that even you would struggle to climb. During the day, the festival and the city beyond is crawling with humans. There is no chance of running through the streets in daylight without being seen and the alarm being raised. It is certain death for you all.'

Asta glanced over to Lipa, wolfing down the eggs rolling into his cage and bashfully smiling with his mouth full at Cosima and Isaac, who chuckled softly as they admired his expression. Tilia looked up, catching Asta's eye, and edged closer, her ears pricking towards the wildcat and the monkey.

'Osborne is going to sell Lipa soon,' Asta went on gravely. 'Men are viewing him and offering more and more money with each visit. We have to get him away from here before it's too late.'

'I will do anything to stop him from falling into cruel human hands,' Tilia added. 'There must be something you can do.'

Just then, Isaac clicked his tongue and motioned for Rosie to join him.

'Please,' Asta implored, seeing the monkey hesitate, 'I have an idea, but it won't work without you.'

'Rosie!' Cosima gently scolded. 'We must go. Come on.'

'I know only one soul who could help,' Rosie said, delaying by slowly clambering down Asta's cage. 'He is the cleverest being I know. I'll bring him to you later tonight.'

With that, the monkey bounded to the floor and disappeared with Cosima and Isaac into the gloom.

Asta and Tilia's eyes met. For the first time, there was hope.

CHAPTER FIFTEEN

JET

From the moment Cosima, Isaac and Rosie departed, Asta and Tilia whispered to one another and planned their escape. In the hours before dawn, while all the other animals were sleeping in their cages, and just as Asta and Tilia were worrying Rosie would not return, a rustle sounded, and Asta and Tilia breathed easier, spying the monkey tentatively creep into the tent with a raven gliding over her head.

Asta's ears pricked in astonishment. 'You're the raven that's been watching me in the baiting ring.' The raven landed and perched upon her cage beside Rosie. Its intelligent eyes looked upon the wildcat as though she was an old friend. Tilia gently untangled herself from Lipa's sleeping embrace and inched closer to the other animals.

'Yes,' the raven croaked softly. 'I've been watching you ever since the hunters brought you and your brother to Rathder's Apothecary Shop on Gunpowder Alley. Wildcats do not belong in a city. Miriam and I have worried about you.'

Asta remembered Miriam staring down at her when she was inside the hunters' wagon. She had been so afraid of her, and of everyone, at that moment, but Asta now realized how different Miriam had been from the other humans she had encountered. A kind of wisdom had glinted in her blue eyes that Asta had not seen in other people.

Rosie introduced the raven fondly. 'This is Jet. He is Miriam's closest friend. I have known them both since I joined Cosima and Isaac many years ago.'

Tilia's brown face scrunched. 'How can a woman be a friend of a raven?'

'Miriam raised me and my brothers and sisters from when we were chicks,' Jet replied warmly, cocking his ebony head towards her.

'If you met Miriam,' Rosie beamed, 'you would agree that if she had the right palate she would be able to speak to us in our own animal tongue.'

'Miriam is not your everyday human.' Jet nodded. 'She is highly sensitive, and she understands and cares deeply about animals, especially those that are suffering. She does what she can, like making the eggs to keep you strong.'

Rosie nodded. 'She has the same concerns for people and gives medicines to those in need.'

'*Medicines.*' Asta remembered the word, and bristled. 'Mad Rathder the apothecary stole my blood and whiskers to make medicines for treating humans.'

'Miriam is different. She is a healer for the ordinary person,' said Jet. 'Most people can't afford a doctor or apothecary. Miriam and her late husband, John, agreed with Nicholas Culpeper. He was a doctor who made it possible for every person, rich or poor, to have access to medical treatment through herbal medicine. Unlike Rathder, all of Miriam's ingredients are homegrown in her garden or foraged from Hampstead Heath, Greenwich or Putney, so her treatments never cost her or her patients anything.'

'She has also influence in the king's court,' Rosie added. 'She is a talented astrologer and the queen has visited Miriam many times, hoping a star reading or a herbal remedy might bring her a child. Every apothecary and astrologer in London envies Miriam for that. Especially Rathder.'

'Rathder has a pet cat, Beauty.' Asta's gut swirled at the thought of her. 'He saved her from the animal killings during the Great Plague.'

'He saved her to serve his own needs.' Jet shook his head. 'Before you arrived at his apothecary shop, Beauty was his source of whiskers, blood and spit for his useless potions. Miriam and I were concerned for her wellbeing at first, but she felt indebted to Rathder for treating her human family when they were dying of the plague and she refused to leave his side. Her bond to him is disturbing. She is not to be trusted. She is his puppet.'

'She has turned my brother, Ash, against me,' Asta mewed sadly. 'It was like watching a spider lure him into a web. Beauty preyed upon his fears of the human world, and made him afraid of the wild too. Now he believes that she and Rathder saved him from certain death. He is too frightened to leave Rathder's house. I have to get back to him. I have to remind him that he belongs in the forest. We will never survive a caged, captive life.'

'Nor will Lipa and I.' Tilia hung her head. 'I will die of a broken heart if he is condemned to a life of torture, like me. He is the only thing that has kept me alive since I was taken from the wild. It is nothing but suffering, being a human plaything. It will break his spirit. I cannot let it happen to him.'

'Miriam and I help as many animals as we can,' Jet said. 'Cockerels from cockfights, badgers from baiting matches, dogs from dog fights, and when the Great Plague struck we sheltered as many dogs and cats we could. Miriam has rehomed many with her patients now. They have brought company to the lonely, comfort to the grief-stricken and laughter to the sad. But we have never rescued bears before. We tried to liberate a mother and her cub from the Hope Theatre ten years ago, but we couldn't cut through the cages as planned. When we returned the following night, we were discovered and John was shot and killed.' Jet's wings hung down with regret, and Rosie laid a sympathetic paw on his back. 'The day after, the Puritans executed the bears to punish men's sins for enjoying the bear-baiting games. There was nothing we could do to stop it.'

'I have a plan,' Asta began, standing tall and staring earnestly at the raven and the monkey. 'But we need your help.'

'Asta,' the raven started, 'we have never succeeded in breaking out any animals from the Bartholomew Fair—'

'I know,' Asta interrupted, aware he was going to repeat what Tilia and Rosie had already told her, 'but did you ever have a brown bear to cause a diversion?' Rosie and Jet looked at one another, their eyes gleaming. 'The gates are locked at night, and the risk of recapture or death is too high for escape during the daylight hours.' The monkey and the raven nodded in agreement. 'But if humans see a large brown bear running free, they will panic. Their only thoughts will be saving their skins. During the distraction, Lipa and I will flee. Wildcats and bears are good climbers. We won't need to run through the streets of London. We'll go over the rooftops where no humans roam.'

'But, Tilia –' Rosie's brow furrowed, turning to the mother bear – 'you can't do that and not be seen. You could lose everything – Lipa, maybe even your life . . .'

'Osborne won't kill me.' Tilia shook her head. 'I'm too valuable to him, especially when there will be no bear cub to replace me. He is motivated by nothing but riches. I am the biggest draw to the baiting matches and the hardest to replace. I don't care what happens to me. Just get Lipa out of here before it's too late, I beg you. If there is another time you can rescue me, then so be it. If I am in shackles forever, I will endure it better, knowing Lipa is free.' Jet and Rosie paused, considering this for a moment. 'If we don't do this,' Tilia went on gravely, 'we will perish.'

'We just need you to open our cages,' Asta added, padding forward and pawing the door to her pen. Jet and Rosie inspected it. It was bolted by a latch that lifted and slid across a large metal plate, making it impossible for any animal to reach from the inside. The raven and the monkey glanced towards Tilia and Lipa's enclosure. It was the same, on a larger scale. 'Then, when Osborne is announcing the start of the baiting matches,' Asta continued, 'Tilia will go into the arena and chase him around the ring. Fear will swiftly spread, and in the commotion Lipa and I will slip away.'

'You and Lipa may not get to the rooftops alive,' Jet said. 'The humans will be terrified of a vicious wildcat and a bear cub on the loose – even more so when they are panicked, and his mother is rampaging through the fair. Many men carry pistols within their coats. All three of you risk getting shot if you do this.'

'I'd rather us die free.' Tilia glanced over at Lipa still peacefully sleeping in their enclosure. 'Even if it only lasts for a moment.'

'Me too,' Asta said. 'There is no life without freedom.'

Jet and Rosie nodded softly. 'We cannot argue with that,' Rosie said, meeting Asta's green eyes staring up at her. 'We all deserve to choose how we live.'

'But the only way this will work,' Jet quickly interjected, 'is if no human sees that these cages have been opened.'

'Osborne's men never check,' Tilia said firmly. 'They only ever open and close them to take us to the baiting ring or return us from it.'

'You must also make sure none of the other animals sleeping behind us now realize what is going to happen.' Jet's eyes roved over them sadly. 'They could raise the alarm and ruin your chances of escape.'

'But if Tilia is fast,' Asta's whiskers drooped on her cheeks, 'she can open their cages with her claws.'

'The element of shock and surprise will be what gives you the advantage,' Rosie said softly. 'Any delay could be disastrous.'

Asta and Tilia looked at the slumbering rats, cockerels and badgers. The thought of leaving them behind made them ache with guilt, knowing the hardships they faced in Osborne's hands.

'There's one last thing you must agree to before we do this,' Jet said, staring earnestly into Asta's open, striated face, and she nodded, hoping with every thump of her heart that he wasn't going to withdraw now. 'If you and Lipa make it out alive, you must come to Miriam's house – you will not survive the city without her aid. Lipa especially is too conspicuous. And, once there, you cannot stray from it, until we say it is safe. If you wander and are seen returning to her home, you put our friends' lives in danger. It is safer for everyone if you are kept in hiding.'

'Lipa will do anything you say,' Tilia replied at once. 'I guarantee it.'

'I cannot live in captivity again.' Asta's ears flattened, a rush of dread skittering through her. 'And I can't leave Ash with Beauty and Rathder any longer. I have to get him out of there and find a way back to the forest . . .'

'It's all right,' Jet reassured, 'Miriam believes in freedom above everything. I guarantee that you will not be caged and she has plenty of space for you to amble. If you can do what we ask, we will help you get your brother back and then rewild you both in time.'

Asta paused, her mind racing, pondering Jet's request and wondering if she could trust him.

'Asta,' Rosie added softly, reading the worry etched across Asta's brow, 'you have to do this because it protects you and others we care for. Isaac and Cosima make no secret of their dislike of baiting animals, and they will be suspected, especially if anyone has seen them secretly feeding you. Miriam will also be in danger. She is Isaac's aunt.'

All Asta wanted was to rescue Ash and return to the forest, but she would never forgive herself if anything happened to those who had been kind to her. If it weren't for Cosima and Isaac's deliveries of Miriam's eggs, and Rosie and Jet's help now, she, Tilia and Lipa would not have had a chance.

'It will not take Osborne and his men long to suspect

foul play,' Rosie went on. 'Your escape and Tilia's attack will cost him dearly, and he will search for someone to blame. We need to keep you in hiding because he will kill Miriam, Cosima and Isaac if he believes they had any part in it.'

Asta's breath caught in her throat. Rathder and Moore were also *Osborne's men*. If they found out that Miriam was sheltering her from the baiting ring, where Asta had been filling their purses and digging them out of debt, Miriam, Isaac and Cosima would be in peril.

'I will do as you ask,' Asta vowed. She turned to Tilia, who was staring fondly at her cub. 'And I promise, whatever happens, I will look after Lipa.'

'As will I.' Tilia smiled, and the sadness in her eyes tightened Asta's throat. In a few hours, Lipa may never see his mother again. Asta knew how that felt.

The bear went on: 'I will do everything I can to look after both of you.' She turned to the raven and the monkey. '*And* your human friends.'

'Then the next time I see you,' Jet said, his dark eyes flicking to Asta, 'will be on the roof of the Priory Church of St Bartholomew the Great. You can see its tower stretching up behind the main tent. Its western Tudor gatehouse is made from timber, wattle and daub, and it is built over a stonework arch that has closed double doors. This will be the hardest to climb, but once you reach the jettied first floor you will be able to straddle the angle and climb up the wooden beams with your claws.'

'And I will catch up with you when you reach Miriam's,' Rosie added. 'Jet and I cannot be seen together when you break free. We are both too identifiable, and we must protect Miriam, Isaac and Cosima. We will open your cages now, but, as soon as we leave, you are on your own.'

Asta and Tilia nodded, hope fluttering in their chests as Jet lifted the latches to Asta's cage with his beak, while Rosie scampered around its metal plate and wriggled and tugged and pulled and pushed the bolt until a soft clang sounded and the fastening slid free. Asta's heart thrummed. She gently pawed the door and looked on, unobstructed, as the raven and the monkey did the same thing to the bears' enclosure. As it clunked open, Jet and Rosie's heads glanced warily at the other baiting animals, but not even Lipa stirred.

The raven and the monkey silently leaped to the ground. 'Good luck,' they whispered, and with a final, doleful glance at the mother bear, shuffling across her enclosure to tightly cradle her cub, they disappeared, leaving Asta and Tilia to wait for the break of day.

CHAPTER SIXTEEN

NOW OR NEVER

Asta and Tilia spent the final hours before the baiting matches commenced tucked up neatly beside the doors of their cages with their paws secretly weighted upon them to ensure they remained closed. Both animals did their best to rest, knowing they would need all the courage and cunning they possessed for the day to come. But Asta felt sick with nerves, and every time she drifted off to sleep she woke with a start, worrying the doors to their cages were ajar. More than once, Asta witnessed Tilia do the same and, when the bear realized she had nothing to fear, she drew her slumbering cub more tightly into her chest. Asta listened to Tilia whisper gentle, loving words to him that Asta wished she could hear from her mother one last time.

Little by little, the tent brightened with sunshine. As

usual, Osborne's men entered the backstage area in the middle of the morning to inspect the baiting ring for repairs and prepare the auditorium for the expected crowds. Asta's green eyes trailed every footstep that trod backstage, and her ears pricked vigilantly whenever a laugh or shout was uttered.

All too soon, the sounds of people muttering and mingling around the fair added to the brouhaha inside the arena that signified the baiting matches were due to begin. The other animals trapped inside their cages jittered uneasily, and Asta steadied her breath as Tilia turned to her, knowing the time to act was almost upon them.

'I've told Lipa what's going to happen,' Tilia whispered. 'And he's promised to do everything you tell him.' The bear looked at her cub, staring up at her devotedly. 'Haven't you, my love?'

Lipa nodded. 'But only until you join us again,' he added, his big, brown eyes twinkling with mischief.

'That's right.' Tilia embraced him. 'I shall not be far behind, and remember that Asta is in charge until I find you.'

Asta's heart tugged, understanding why Tilia was lying to him. He would never leave her side if he realized she could not follow them. Tilia and Asta's eyes met through the bars of their cages, and they smiled softly at one another.

Asta was going to miss her, and she swore to herself she would find a way to reunite the bears.

At that moment, Osborne strode into the backstage area dressed in his fine clothes and swinging his sliver-topped cane theatrically by his side. He sauntered into the arena, followed by the two men that delivered the animals in and out of the baiting ring, and the auditorium roared with wild cheers and whoops as the sense of anticipation mounted in the air.

'This is it,' Tilia said urgently, giving Lipa one final kiss on the head. 'Be a good boy, my darling. Follow Asta, and *promise* me that you won't look back.' He nuzzled into her chest, and Asta looked on, wishing they didn't have to say goodbye. 'It's all right, Asta,' Tilia whispered firmly, reading her expression and smiling kindly. 'Now go – go!'

Asta and the bears flung open the doors of their cages and leaped forward. Instantly, the other animals jolted with surprise and pleaded for their freedom too. Tilia barrelled towards them, and with almighty swipes of her massive paws she liberated as many as she could. In seconds, rats, cockerels and badgers spilled on to the ground.

Tilia bounded towards the arena, her eyes blazing with life. 'The only way out is through the ring!' she bellowed. 'Follow me!'

Together, the animals galloped into the auditorium behind the brown bear.

Cries of alarm went up through the audience as soon as Tilia entered the ring. At once, Osborne pivoted on his heel. He stumbled backwards, momentarily paralysed with fright, but as Tilia roared Osborne's face contorted with malice, and he raised his silver-topped cane to his shoulder to strike her when she neared. A second later, the bear hurtled into him and screams spread through the crowd as she knocked him flat on his back.

'Run as fast as you can, Lipa!' Asta cried, overtaking them, and Lipa obeyed, trailing close behind her. The wildcat glanced back, checking he was there, and her eyes widened.

Osborne was pinned to the ground and slamming his cane against Tilia's body. In defence, she wrapped her jaws about his arm and tossed him from side to side, flinging the stick from his grasp and hurling the periwig from his head. The violence of it sent a wave of panic surging across the auditorium. Men and women blurred as they hurried out of their seats and clambered over one another to escape the tent. Some tumbled over the raised tiered seats and landed heavily into the baiting ring, while others leaped down to it on purpose and sprinted for their lives. Moore and Rathder jostled through the scrum, shoving and elbowing every man, woman or child out of their way to join the stampede, trampling any unfortunate person that had fallen.

Asta and Lipa raced on, dodging tankards, stones and debris being pelted in their direction, and bounded past legs frantically careering across their paths. The humans shrieked whenever they veered towards the smaller bear, and others squealed, recognizing the ferocious wildcat that had grown to be a notorious attraction of the fair. In the confusion, the cockerels, rats and badgers had disappeared in the crush, and Asta hoped they would survive as she guided Lipa onward along the route she remembered taking with Moore when he first brought her to Osborne, the morning after Beauty had torn her from Ash.

Through the pandemonium, Asta spied the wrought-iron gates where Moore had pushed aside the children trying to catch a glimpse of the acrobats on the eve of the fair. This time, they were open and overflowing with a deluge of people escaping the arena.

'This way, Lipa!' Asta panted, swerving to the left and the bear cub sped after her.

It was as Asta and Lipa left the main tent and felt the warmth of the sun on their faces that they heard shots being fired. Wails of fear hollered all around them, and Asta blanched, worrying deeply for Tilia. But she didn't have

time to feel. She had to get Lipa to safety as she had promised.

Asta halted for a moment inside the rolling tide of humans. She looked up at the rooftops, her head darting left and right, searching for the church tower. Lipa hunched close, and his ears flattened as he flinched among the throng of fleeing people.

'Over there!' Asta cried as she saw the crenelated steeple of the Priory Church of St Bartholomew the Great looming up behind the main tent. A black silhouette of a raven stretched its wings against the clear blue sky on its spire. 'Come on!'

Asta and Lipa raced towards it. Zigzagging through the crowds, past abandoned stalls, colourful flags, overturned crates and discarded cuts of pork and half-eaten apples, the wildcat and the bear cub soon arrived at the tall Tudor gatehouse built over a stonework church arch with closed double doors, just as Jet had described.

'We can't climb this,' Asta yowled, leaping up with Lipa, again and again, trying to gain purchase with their claws, but it was hopeless. The stones were too large and too flat. Asta's insides swirled with panic, and her gaze flitted all around them, hunting for something to climb. A horse strapped into a hay wain stood to their left, nervously swishing its tail as it watched the furore spread across the fair. The back of the cart was open, and it was aligned beneath the jettied corner of the timber gatehouse's first floor.

'Quick!' Asta motioned her head to it, and Lipa understood what she was thinking.

The wildcat dashed to the wagon and leaped inside it with a *poof* of hay, closely followed by the bear cub, who lifted himself to the same place with a clumsy kick of his hind legs. Together, they shuffled through the pile of golden strands and clambered on to the rim of the wain that creaked under Lipa's weight.

Asta and Lipa were balancing there unsteadily and craning their necks upwards towards the building overhead when the horse cocked its ears warily and swerved its head towards them. With a snort of alarm and a stamp of its hoof, the horse bolted forward.

'Jump, Lipa!' Asta yelled.

The wildcat and the bear cub hurled themselves upright. A moment later, their front claws scratched against the black timbers of the gatehouse and Asta and Lipa dug them deep into the wood.

Instinct hummed through their veins and they scaled the building as though it was a tree in the wild. Just as Jet had said, the climb was easier once they'd straddled the corner of the jettied first and second floors, and soon Asta and Lipa hauled themselves on to the pitched gatehouse roof. Panting and trembling from the climb, they scrabbled over its roof and clambered down the other side.

*

Amidst the crush of people below, Rathder and Moore stood rooted to the ground and stared at the Tudor gatehouse. They scowled, watching the wildcat and the bear cub disappear from view, and their faces darkened with fury as a familiar black raven launched itself from the neighbouring church spire and glided through the air to meet them.

CHAPTER SEVENTEEN

MIRIAM

Asta and Lipa immediately felt calmer, leaving the hullaballoo on the other side of the Tudor gatehouse. Behind its closed double doors, the Priory of St Bartholomew the Great stood at the end of a stone walkway leading to the western entrance of the church. Dark green ivy crept over a stone arch, and a tall, leafy plane tree overlooked a small graveyard. No people roamed here, and the wildcat and the bear felt the first flutter of freedom as they watched the raven glide from the high church spire and land on the roof beside them.

'I wasn't sure you had it in you,' Jet clacked, his ebony eyes glinting with friendliness as Asta and Lipa lay on their sides and tried to catch their breaths. 'Now is not the time to rest.' The raven's feathers fluffed around his neck. 'Come with me!'

Jet uttered four excited clicking sounds, burst into the air and swiftly disappeared over the rooftops to the right. Asta and Lipa stared at one another with a gasp of alarm. They jumped to the neighbouring building and raced after the raven, their paws scratching against the roof tiles, hope thumping in their limbs.

Asta and Lipa had never marvelled at the human world until then. Houses unfurled in every direction amongst a scattering of lofty church-bell towers and pointed spires, stretching above horse-drawn carts, carriages and people meandering through the streets below. But it was a building to the south that made them pause with wonder. An enormous cathedral loomed over the city, higher than anything Asta had ever seen before. Its ornate rows of Gothic windows and pinnacles were imposing, and its larger decorative windows were as intricate as the underside of a leaf. Its long, rectangular tower stood tall above four slate roofs positioned in the shape of a cross, and the structure was enveloped in timber scaffolding, giving Asta the impression of viewing it through a dense wood of trees. A shiver scuttled over her. She couldn't fathom how humans had constructed it and the rest of the city that swept over distances further than she could see. Animals didn't stand a chance against the human mind, and she would never feel safe until she left their world.

London's buildings were packed together, and their jettied upper floors made the roofs almost touch, making it easy for Asta and Lipa to bound from one to the next and chase Jet southwards towards the Thames. The river glittered in the afternoon sunshine below rows of houses overlooking deep banks of cracked mud from a stone floodwall. It wasn't long before they reached the Thames, and Asta and Lipa followed Jet to the blackened ruins of a house that had recently been destroyed by a fire. They clambered down its scorched woodwork to hurry after the raven flying swiftly alongside the water to the west.

As the wildcat and the bear cub bounded upstream along the wall, Asta watched the water ripple and swirl. It was not like the clear, rushing river she knew from her forest where her mother had scooped passing fish on to its shores for her and Ash to eat. This river smelt rotten. It was murky and thick, and had chewed apple cores, animal dung and discarded vegetable tops bobbing beside distant passenger ferries, transporting humans past barges carrying coal and grain, and smaller dinghies that were rowed by watermen, hauling people through the city by the tug of their oars. Asta frowned. Humans had completely possessed the river, from encasing its shoreline to polluting its waters.

'Come on, Lipa.' Asta glanced over her shoulder at the bear cub cantering at her heels, and a determined growl rose in her throat as she spurred herself onward. 'The sooner we reach Miriam's, the sooner we can find our way back to the forest.'

They followed the water shimmering in the afternoon sunlight despite the filth churning beneath the rippling tide until the buildings thinned and the floodwall descended into the dried mud. Ahead, Jet soared over a sailboat moored to a small dock with wooden decking. The dock led to a filigree gate that was left ajar within a tall, broad brick wall. Above it, thick treetops rustled in the breeze, and Asta and Lipa beamed as the raven swerved sharply towards them and vanished inside the leafy boughs.

The wildcat and the bear cub scrambled up the dock's wooden poles and rushed along the deck to the gate. Asta slowed to tentatively scan the garden beyond, but Lipa overtook her and barrelled through the gap in the gate. It blew open and, with a leap of surprise, Asta galloped after him into a vast, bright, open space.

Joy skittered through them as they felt their paws sink into the crisp, mossy grass. Mature, verdant trees grew all around them, and although it wasn't the forest she craved Asta had never felt happier, seeing leaves flutter against the sky again. She closed her eyes and inhaled deeply, her senses blazing as she breathed in the familiar scents of oak, holly, elm, daisy, willow, poppy, bramble, foxglove and gorse, and her nose tingled, smelling olive, honeysuckle, sunflower and other plants, trees and flowers she had never encountered before.

To the west, the huge garden was made up of parched lawn, flowerbeds and organized herb and vegetable beds, with six bell-shaped beehives situated to the east. Directly ahead, a modest house covered in wilted creepers stood towards the northern wall. Its windows were flung open to invite the breeze inside, and a line of humans snaked round a corner into a side door. The house was surrounded by paving stones where a whippet and a white terrier lay, their flanks rising and falling as they basked in the sunshine and ignored a flock of chickens foraging for ants and scratching the ground for worms. Asta froze. An old, greying mastiff, identical to the hounds with whom she had so recently brawled, paced around the queue of people, who shifted nervously as it sniffed their ankles and unremarkable clothes.

'Welcome to Miriam's house,' Jet said, swooping down from an oak tree. 'Don't forget, you must both stay hidden.' His eyes snapped to the humans on the other side of the garden. 'A bear cub in London is not a sight you forget, even more so when it has a wildcat as a travelling companion. We don't want anyone we don't know to see you. Osborne's men will be looking for you after the mayhem you caused at the fair. Follow me.'

It was as a mother protectively lifted her young child to her hip and shooed the mastiff away that the dog caught sight of Asta and Lipa ducking into the thicket to the south. The old dog barked at once, and the other dogs immediately followed its gaze.

Asta and Lipa stared wide-eyed as the group of dogs charged towards them with their hackles stiffening. Asta pushed Lipa deep into the shrub and shielded his body with hers. She bared her claws and faced the approaching hounds with a ferocious growl.

The pack of dogs were almost upon them when Jet flew from the undergrowth and swooped over the mastiff's head.

'Stop!' he shrieked. 'The bear cub and the wildcat are not intruders. They have just escaped the baiting ring like you once did.'

The dogs halted, their ears pricking. 'They're on the run?' the mastiff asked, scouring the shrub with her dark eyes. Asta crept forward, eager to hear their conversation.

The raven nodded. 'The bear's mother caused a diversion

and they fled the Bartholomew Fair.'

The dogs' faces fell. All the animals in London feared the brutality of the brawls there, and none was safe from it. The humans had pitted every creature against one another over the years. Very few lived past the first match, and almost none saw the end of the festival.

'They survived the fair?' the small white terrier at the mastiff's ankle asked incredulously.

'So far.' Jet nodded. 'But they need our help.' The raven's gaze wandered over the queue of humans. 'We cannot draw any attention to them. It will put Miriam in danger. They were valuable commodities, and men will be hunting for them.'

The dogs' ears pulled back with worry.

'Miriam must be warned,' the mastiff said gravely.

'She will know what to do,' Jet replied. 'She rescued you; she can save Asta and Lipa too.'

At that moment, a loud yell sounded. Asta, Lipa, Jet and the dogs glanced towards it at once and scowled, watching two men barge through the queue of people, storm into Miriam's house and slam the door behind them.

Asta swallowed.

Rathder and Moore had found them.

CHAPTER EIGHTEEN

RATHDER AND MOORE

The humans and the chickens scattered as the pack of dogs bolted to the house and barked incessantly with wrinkled noses and lips pulled back from their teeth.

'Stay here.' Jet's feathers ruffled anxiously all over his body. Lipa moved closer to Asta, who was hunched to the ground behind the shrub, her green eyes blazing in the dappled light. 'If they find you, Miriam will be blamed, and the consequences will be severe.'

Jet charged from the undergrowth and soared through the air towards the house. Asta's fur stiffened as she watched the raven swoop over the dogs, scratching and burrowing at the closed door, and vanish through an open ground-floor window where three figures blustered inside.

Every sinew in Asta's body urged her to take Lipa and flee from Rathder and Moore, but there was nowhere for them to go. What freedom they had now was fragile. Lipa was a big bear cub and would not go unnoticed in a city heaving with humans. Their return to the wild rested solely on a raven and his human friend. Without their help, their chance of escaping London was slim. She and Lipa could quickly be recaptured. Then she would never see Ash again, and Tilia would have sacrificed herself for nothing. Asta shook the temptation to run away now from her head. It was a risk she couldn't take, and if Rathder and Moore harmed Miriam, she and Lipa might be stuck in London forever.

A large crash sounded from within Miriam's house, and a rush of worry and fury swept through Asta, remembering Miriam's kind face staring down at her when she'd first arrived at Rathder's Apothecary Shop. Miriam didn't deserve Rathder and Moore's wrath.

Lipa cowered, staring through the thicket. 'Who are those men?'

Asta glowered. 'The thin one with the long beard is Rathder. He bought me and my brother, Ash, from hunters who stole us from our forest so he could use our blood and whiskers for his potions that he sells to his customers.' Her voice wavered. 'My brother is still trapped inside his house.' Lipa shuffled closer, and the warmth of his body filled

Asta with calm. 'The other man is Moore. He's Rathder's business partner. He's a brute. Both are driven by greed. They took me to the Bartholomew Fair.'

A cold, bristling silence descended as they stared at the dogs digging at the door. Asta despised Rathder and Moore. She'd like nothing more than to see the dogs give them a taste of their own medicine. But no matter how much the dogs jumped and snapped and scratched, they were never going to get to them through the closed door. The timber was thick, and the door handle was made from a heavy ring of iron that no paws could operate. Asta frowned, her mind whirring.

It was then that a woman's voice shrieked from within the house.

'Lipa,' she growled, 'we can't let anything happen to Miriam; she's our only hope of returning to the forest. We need to get those men out of her house, so she is safe.'

'But how?' Lipa shook his head. 'If we're seen, we'll be taken back to the fair.'

Asta scanned the garden, and she breathed easier, seeing that all the other humans had fled. She looked at the building. From the open ground-floor window, she glimpsed Rathder and Moore, looming over Miriam and ducking as Jet fiercely flapped his wings from where he perched on her shoulder. The raven had got to her by flying through this window. If the dogs could get in the same way, Rathder and Moore would be gone. Asta's gaze searched the garden again. Beside the house, a felled tree was lying on its side with an axe biting into its bark above a pile of logs. She had seen beavers in the forest roll similar trunks to their dams. It was too big for her to push by herself, but with Lipa's aid, they could move it under the window and then the dogs could use it to vault inside.

She turned to Lipa and the bear cub's ears pricked eagerly, listening to Asta's plan. 'Then all we have to do,' she went on, 'is hide in the thicket and watch Rathder and Moore flee from the dogs.'

Lipa nodded with enthusiasm, and Asta smiled.

With a final glance at the house from beneath the shrub, Asta stepped into the open air and galloped to the broad oak tree with Lipa following closely from behind. The wildcat and the bear cub crouched there before dashing to a flowerbed and continuing towards the house behind a dense screen of tall grasses.

They arrived at the tree trunk, and their ears flattened. The commotion from within the house was loud and clear now. Asta and Lipa stared up at the open window, fearing the scene inside, before pawing the felled tree. Asta was the first to leap against it, and when Lipa did the same it began to roll towards the house.

'Miriam, you Dutch swine.' Moore's low, furious tone made Asta and Lipa tensed with fright. 'For the last time: give us the bear cub and the wildcat *now*. We saw your mangey raven help them escape over the rooftops.'

'My raven has been here all day,' Miriam replied. 'Your imagination is getting the better of you, Moore. How do you suppose a human could organize such a thing?'

'Witchcraft,' Moore sneered. 'You control the mind of that bird. It does your bidding. It's well known.'

'Nonsense!' Miriam laughed. 'All I am known for is being a widow, a herbalist and an astrologer who treats her patients for free, unlike you, Marcus Rathder, who masquerades as an apothecary and star reader to exploit others for financial gain.'

'You are also known to be the widow of a criminal who was shot trying to steal bears from the Hope Theatre,' Rathder snapped. Hearing his voice again made Asta's fur stiffen along her spine.

'Lies,' Miriam scoffed, 'John was feeding the bears. He was never convicted of a crime.'

'Defend him until you have no breath left, Miriam,'

Rathder scoffed. 'We know the truth. You are as guilty as he was.'

'Prove it, then.' Miriam countered. There was a pause as Rathder could think of nothing to say.

'Foreigners like you with inherited wealth should be careful,' Rathder said at last. 'England is at war with Holland, and that makes you untrustworthy. It wouldn't take much for us to convince the public you were anything we wanted them to think you were, and while London may not believe in witchcraft as much as the provinces these days, witches still swing from the gallows when they are found. You have wanted my wildcat since you first spied her outside my apothecary shop – you shall not get away with this thievery!'

'Your threats don't scare me,' Miriam retorted firmly, 'for I have neither the wildcat *nor* the bear cub of which you speak. The only animals you'll find here are my dogs, chickens and ravens, and none of them has come from the Bartholomew Fair.'

'But you detest the baiting matches there, don't you, Miriam?' Moore hissed, 'You've stolen dogs, badgers and cockerels from the fighting ring so your precious animals wouldn't come to any harm.'

'Get your facts straight, Moore,' Miriam sighed irritably.

'I *bought* those creatures to give them better lives.'

'And you took in cats and dogs when they were being culled for spreading the plague last year, didn't you?' Rathder jeered. 'You spread the pestilence and should be punished.'

'Much like you and that cat you have roaming through your quack apothecary shop,' Miriam rebutted. 'For heaven's sake, Rathder,' she chuckled. 'You cannot frighten me because I know nothing about the missing animals you seek.'

'We saw that raven meet the wildcat and the bear cub!' Moore flared, and Asta and Lipa startled beneath the window as the sound of his fist thundered against a table. 'We know it was you, and we will make sure you will be punished for the mayhem you caused at the fair! We'll get you for it – and soon. You'll see! It won't be long before you answer to the wrath of London!'

'That's it,' Asta whispered as she and Lipa finally positioned the trunk under the open window. It wouldn't be easy, but the dogs could use it to vault inside the house. 'Now, we just need to fetch the others.'

Asta and Lipa beamed as they turned and scampered a short way over to the dogs. The barking and burrowing ceased for a moment, the dogs looking from the wildcat and the bear cub to the tree trunk, before they charged at full speed behind Asta and Lipa, who led them back to the open window.

'Like I said,' they heard Miriam say calmly, despite the tension in the air, 'I do not know anything about what happened at the Bartholomew Fair.'

'Fine!' Moore raged in reply. 'I'll tell you what happened! Somebody let the great Carpathian bear loose to rampage through the baiting arena. She killed Osborne and started a stampede before I shot her dead.' Asta and Lipa froze. 'With *this*!'

CHAPTER NINETEEN

MIRIAM'S KITCHEN

Before Moore could draw the pistol, the mastiff hurtled through the open window with the three other dogs chasing her from behind.

'Come on, Lipa!' Asta turned to the bear cub, paralysed with grief. She pushed her head against his shoulder, but he remained rooted to the ground. 'We have to hide. If we're seen, Miriam will be blamed, and we'll be recaptured!'

Just then, the last dog jumped free of the felled tree, and Asta yowled in pain as the force of the vaulting dog pushed the tree trunk on to her hind paw.

She drew a sharp breath and tried to pull it free. 'Lipa!' she wailed, panic seizing her voice.

The terrifying uproar from within the house snapped the bear cub out of his trance. He met Asta's petrified gaze and hurled his weight against the felled tree.

Asta winced to a stand, her paw throbbing.

Lipa pressed his head against hers. 'Are you all right?'

Asta could barely hear him over the cacophony of smashing furniture, barks, shouts, snarls and squawks blaring from the open window above their heads.

'Hurry,' she urged, and they limped away as fast as Asta could manage. 'It won't be long before—'

A loud bang sounded and the wildcat and bear cub blanched. Leaping in alarm, they hobbled through the tall grasses and crouched low to watch. Miriam's door had burst open and slammed against the wall. Rathder and Moore dashed from it and sprinted at full pelt from the dogs. In seconds, they had disappeared behind the house, and a few moments later Asta and Lipa no longer heard the racket of barking hounds and listened instead to the wind sigh in the trees.

Although Asta's plan had worked, she and Lipa didn't speak. Now that the furore had passed, the silence was unsettling. They cowered in the grass and waited, not knowing what to do next.

It wasn't long before Miriam stormed from the house with Jet perched upon her shoulder.

'Barbarians!' she huffed to the raven as she marched past the wildcat and the bear cub. She stomped across the lawn towards the small gate that led to the river, with her fist clutched around Moore's pistol and her skirts swishing with her strides. On reaching the gate, she hurled the gun over her shoulder towards the water, spun on her heels and headed back to the house.

'And they called *me* swine!' She shook her head indignantly, and Jet cawed in outrage. His ebony head darted around the garden and checked for any more threats. 'There aren't enough words to describe what monsters those men are! Rathder is a criminal who forged his qualifications and profited during the plague by selling poisonous concoctions to the afflicted. Then he plundered the belongings of the dead as soon as they passed away.'

Asta's fur tingled. Beauty had lied.

'And Moore,' Miriam spat, the name offending her tongue. She wrung her hands together, trying to stop them trembling at the thought of him. 'He is a cruel, heartless menace who terrorizes anyone he sees fit,' she scoffed in disgust. 'And now wildcats are in the baiting ring. Those shy, elusive creatures will perish without a forest.' Miriam swallowed. 'And that poor mother bear. It must have been protecting her young. What happened at the fair was a tragedy, not a conspiracy.' She sighed sadly. 'Just like what happened to Blind Bess and my John.'

Miriam was halfway through her rant when Jet caught sight of two unblinking pairs of eyes, peeking through the tall blades of grass.

He launched from Miriam's shoulder and fluttered to the lawn. 'I told you not to move from the shrub!' the raven admonished, parting the long grasses with his beak and stepping inside Asta and Lipa's hiding place. 'Rathder and Moore were right here, prowling for both of you, and if they'd found you Miriam would have been in great peril.'

'We know, Jet,' Asta countered. 'We couldn't let them hurt her, so we pushed that tree trunk under the window for the dogs to get inside and chase them away.'

Jet's head swung towards the house. 'Then thank you.' He exhaled deeply. 'When Moore pulled out that pistol –' he paused, his feathers ruffling around his neck – 'I dreaded what would happen. That man is unpredictable. Others have not been so lucky.'

It was then that Miriam's gentle, oval face tentatively appeared above them and she gasped as she spied the wildcat and the bear cub. 'So you *did* help them, Jet?' She smiled.

Asta and Lipa flinched and bolted further into the

grasses, but as Asta pressed upon her hind paw, she tumbled and yowled. Lipa stood over her and growled fiercely at the woman who had startled them.

Jet hopped to them. 'It's all right,' Jet reassured. 'She didn't mean to frighten you.' Asta and Lipa said nothing and peered at Miriam suspiciously, both wary of being so close to a human being again. 'Not all people are bad. Cosima and Isaac helped you at the fair, remember? And I wouldn't have brought you here if you wouldn't be safe with her.'

'You are one of Rathder's wildcats I saw a few weeks ago, aren't you?' Miriam asked. 'Don't worry. I won't let him get his hands on you again.' Miriam's gaze shifted to Lipa. 'Or you, you dear thing.' She paused, her blue eyes misting for a moment. 'I just wish we could have helped your mother too.'

Lipa hunched lower in the grasses. Asta curled up beside him, her tail twitching.

'Rewild! Rewild!' Jet croaked.

Asta's jaw slackened, astonished that he could speak human.

'Yes . . .' Miriam nodded. 'We must – and soon. I won't be able to keep you here for long. Rathder and Moore won't wait before coming back, and this young bear cub is already so big. If you grow much more, I won't be able to conceal you in my cart or my boat.' She bit her lip as she thought. 'Where to rehome you is the next puzzle. Bears haven't roamed Britain for hundreds of years.'

'Forest! Forest!' Jet cawed.

'Of course,' Miriam affirmed. 'But where? Hampstead? Richmond? Thetford? Hunters scour those woods. Some almost fired at me once. That's why I wear my red cloak and sing during my trips there.' She chuckled. 'And it's such fun, scaring off their prey,' she added before crossing her arms, lifting her hand to her face and tapping her cheek with a ponderous finger. 'It has to be somewhere where you will not be found.' She drew a deep, determined breath. 'I must think, but first –' she stared at Asta – 'I need to look at that leg. You may not survive the wild if it's not seen to. I will make a remedy for it. Bring them to me if you can, Jet. I'll be in my workshop.'

Miriam turned away and quietly talked to herself as she paced back to the house.

'She's right, you know.' Jet bent towards Asta's hind paw. The wildcat drew it closer to her, not trusting anyone near it. 'You need your wits and your health to make it in the wild. An injury like that makes you vulnerable. You won't last long if you can't run away from danger.' He stepped towards the lawn. 'Come with me to Miriam's workshop. She will know what to do.'

Asta's hackles stiffened. 'I won't go inside another human house,' she growled. 'I don't belong there. I can stay in this garden and rest. I'll be fine.'

'Then you risk recapture and death,' Jet said over his shoulder. 'And good luck catching any food with only three good legs too.'

Asta's ears flattened. She hadn't thought of that. It had been so long since she had tried to hunt, and it had been difficult enough when she wasn't hurt. 'Miriam has plenty of food inside,' Jet continued. 'Most of her patients donate it in exchange for her treatments. We get plenty of eggs from the chickens as well.' Lipa's ears twitched, and the raven continued with a shrewd smile: 'There's more than enough to go round. Even more, while the dogs are gone.'

Asta looked at the bear cub sitting heavily on his bottom, staring at the ground. His body drooped with grief from his whiskers to his paws. Asta knew there was nothing she could say to make him feel better. A lump still rose in her throat each time she remembered she would never see her mother again. Like Lipa, she never had a chance to say goodbye.

'Letting Miriam help you doesn't mean you are betraying

the wild, Asta,' Jet said softly. 'She doesn't want to make you her pet. She wants you to be free, and the stronger you are, the better chance you and Lipa have staying that way. Isn't that what his mother died for?'

Lipa uttered a long, shuddering sigh. Asta pressed her head against his chest and wished she could take his pain away. She thought of Tilia and Ash. Jet was right and, as much as she disliked the human world, she needed Miriam's help, now more than ever, if they were going to find their way home.

'Come on, Lipa.' She nuzzled his shoulder, and the bear cub's doleful face slowly turned to hers. 'The sooner we go, the sooner we leave.'

Jet led the way into the house through the same side door that Asta and Lipa had watched Rathder and Moore flee from not long before. Asta and Lipa hovered at the entrance with their noses low to the ground and their ears twitching on their heads.

'She won't bite,' Jet chuckled, watching them edge across the sun-drenched threshold. The raven hopped ahead, his talons quietly clacking against a stone-floored corridor that was cloaked in shadow. Asta limped forward with Lipa slowly padding by her side.

The first thing Asta noticed was the smell. Rathder's house had reeked of opium, preserving fluid and tobacco; Miriam's smelled earthy, floral and warm. The further they trod, the more pungent the scents became, and as Jet rounded a corner they arrived at the heart of Miriam's home.

It was a large, chaotic room with a dark row of beams across the ceiling and panelled, wooden walls that were covered in botanical and anatomical drawings. A spinning wheel was lying on the floor beside a loom with a torn weave in the far corner. Three windows opened out to the garden, and each one had tendrils of ivy creeping inside that fanned up the walls to the ceiling. In the middle of the room was a vast bricked fireplace where a cauldron bubbled over bright embers and a dome of dough baked inside the mouth of a deep, arched opening to the side of the inglenook. In the hearth, overturned buckets spilled puddles of coloured water on to the wooden floor. Above them, wool dripped from a line hung from the oak mantel alongside generous bunches of lavender, rosemary, poppies, sage, bay and thyme.

Miriam hummed to herself while she picked yellow arnica and white camomile petals and ground them together with a pestle and mortar at the far end of a long table that stretched the length of the room. At its centre, a knocked over fruit bowl had scattered apples, figs, plums, pears and grapes all over the room.

'Welcome.' She glanced up at Asta and Lipa, hesitating at the entrance and peeking round the corner from the safety of the corridor. 'Your medicine will be ready in a minute.'

Miriam turned behind her where shelves carried copious ceramic pots finely labelled *Elder Leaves*, *Fenugreek*, *Linseed*, *Gorse*, *Fennel*, *Rose* and *Borage* stood among jars of honey, crab-apple and berry preserves. She picked two vessels marked *Ground Hawthorn Flowers* and *Willow Bark* and added a handful of each to her mixture with a generous dribble of oil from an ornate jug, before pouring the contents over a thick chopping board that was covered with cuts of mutton.

She combined the two, and Jet fluttered up to Miriam's worktop and pecked at the meat.

'Stop that, you greedy cur,' she chided, and the raven hopped away with a lump of gristle. She chuckled as he flew to the windowsill. 'That's for our guests.'

Asta and Lipa continued to linger and stared at the upturned room. 'I will clear up Rathder's and Moore's mess later,' Miriam said firmly, taking a pinch of *Betony* and sprinkling it on her ingredients. 'I must fix the inflammation in your paw first.' She ducked below the table and reappeared with two bowls that she filled with the meat. Asta and Lipa backed away as she walked towards them and placed them on the floor a few feet away. She paused there for a moment and sighed. 'I also need to take those collars from your necks.' A growl rose in Asta's throat. She would not let a human touch her again.

'Those shackles are a beacon for anyone searching for you,' Jet said firmly, 'and you cannot take them to the wild. Let her release you. Why would Miriam hurt you when she is doing everything she can to help you?'

Asta stared up at Miriam and the knot in her gut eased. Jet was right – she didn't need to fear this woman. Asta slowly edged closer and Lipa followed.

Miriam inched forward. Reaching behind their necks with rough, floral-scented hands, she swiftly pulled out the pins fixing the collars together and stepped away. The steel fell from Asta and Lipa's necks and clanged as the shackles hit the floor. The wildcat and bear cub sniffed them, their noses wrinkling.

'Now,' Miriam said, and smiled, 'we have to find a way of getting you somewhere safe.'

It was as she stepped to the fireplace and righted the

buckets and the spinning wheel when they heard fists thumping hard on Miriam's front door.

Everyone jumped, their heads darting towards the sound. With a gasp, Miriam snatched the bowls of meat, raced back towards the fireplace and urgently stamped her foot on a soot-covered brick in the hearth. At once, the back wall slid away to the left and opened a secret doorway to a small chamber beyond.

'Jet, get them in here – now – and close the entrance behind you!' She swiftly strode away. 'I'll do my best to stall whoever that is.'

The pounding began again. 'Come on!' Jet squawked, launching from the windowsill and landing beside Asta and Lipa. Neither bear nor wildcat wanted to go further into Miriam's house, but the threat of facing whoever was at the door made them trot briskly after the raven. As soon as they crossed the threshold of the secret room, Jet jumped and snatched a cord dangling in the shadows in his beak. Tugging it with a forceful flap of his wings, the doorway creaked closed and sealed the raven, the wildcat and the bear cub inside.

CHAPTER TWENTY

THREE DAYS

'What is this place?' Asta asked, crouching beside Lipa with her green eyes wandering around the small room, hidden behind the fireplace. Daylight shone from a disused chimney pot above onto a large celestial globe, decorated with gold stars and lines that passed through animals, mythical creatures and human beings. The walls were lined with books and snuffed-out candles, and every surface was covered with papers scribbled with notes and diagrams of comets, a white building with four towers, ravens and star charts.

'It's a priest hole where Catholics once hid from those who wanted to harm them, more than a hundred years ago,' Jet whispered, as he hopped towards one of several dots of light. He pressed his eye against it and was able to see into Miriam's workshop. 'Miriam uses this place as her secret office.' He nodded to a dresser behind them, stuffed with books. 'A concealed passageway lies behind those shelves, which leads to the river. I'll—'

Asta, Lipa and the raven froze, hearing voices and footsteps nearby. The voices did not belong to Rathder and Moore, as they had feared, but to a man and a woman, speaking rapidly.

'It's Cosima, Isaac and Rosie,' Jet croaked.

Asta and Lipa shuffled to the raven and joined him, looking through peepholes in the fireplace, to watch Cosima and Isaac's conversation with Miriam.

Miriam heaved a sigh of relief. 'Goodness, nephew, you scared me bursting in like that. Look at me, I'm shaking. What is the matter?'

'The Bartholomew Fair has been closed for the rest of the season.' Isaac took the restless monkey, wriggling on his shoulder, and placed her on Miriam's long table. Rosie nosed around the fruit bowl, lifted a fig to her mouth and nibbled it, her dark eyes flitting around the room. She put it down and plucked a grape instead. 'Osborne was killed by his own baiting bear,' Isaac continued. 'The animal cages backstage had been sabotaged.'

Rosie's gaze flicked guiltily towards Miriam for a moment before she crept to the end of the table, hopped to the floor and explored the room.

'I heard,' Miriam replied, bending and picking up the knocked-over buckets, her hands still trembling a little. She untied her apron from her waist and used it to mop up the puddle of coloured water that had collected around the hearth. 'Rathder and Moore were here before, searching for their escaped wildcat and a bear cub.'

'They are yet to be found,' Isaac noted. 'Most of the other animals have not been so lucky.'

'I worried they knew about the medicinal eggs I made for you,' Miriam turned to him and her eyes twinkled with pride. 'Did you open the cages?'

'No!' Cosima's face went ashen at the suggestion. Rosie quickly slunk away from the fireplace and busied herself with weave in the loom, 'If anyone saw us delivering the eggs, we could be accused of doing so. They would likely suspect you, Isaac's aunt, were behind it.' Cosima swallowed, stepping towards Miriam, who was wringing her sodden apron into a bucket and creaking to a stand.

Isaac nodded gravely. 'Many people remember your campaigns to end the baiting matches, and how hard you and Uncle John tried to save Blind Bess and all the other fighting bears. You are well known for rescuing animals from harm.'

'That is true, but how could they believe an old woman like me could have done something like this?'

'It doesn't matter whether you could have done it or not. A fortune has been lost,' Isaac said. 'Every stall-holder, performer, investor, artist and ticket distributor relies on the fair for money each year. They are furious and afraid, and looking for someone to blame.'

'But they cannot make me responsible.' Miriam waved the worry away as she returned to the fireplace and removed the cauldron from the heat. She took it to her worktop, poured hot water into an earthenware teapot, and placed a handful of camomile flowers inside it. 'I've not left my house or garden for days, and patients have been coming and going since first thing this morning . . .'

'But can anyone confirm your whereabouts last night?' Cosima interrupted.

Miriam clinked the teapot lid into place. 'I am a widow. I live alone. I stargaze at night, and by day I treat the sick, and tend to my garden. They will soon realize it had nothing to do with me.'

'But, all the same, you are in danger until the animals are found,' Isaac said. 'We heard some say you could not be trusted because you're Dutch, and England is at war with Holland.'

'That old nonsense again!' Miriam retorted. 'I was married to your uncle, who was as English as you, Isaac. These people could say the same things about you, Cosima, for being a Catholic. Outsiders are always the first to be blamed.' She collected three tumblers from her shelf and put them next to the teapot with a hurt sigh. 'London is home to people of different origins and faiths, and, while England has many enemies, the three of us do not number among them. But we must be careful. Nobody is safe when the ignorant population spread lies and hysteria. Take care of your thoughts, my dears. Anxiety breeds anxiety. It's more infectious than the plague if you let it run wild. We need to keep our wits about us.'

She poured the camomile infusion and handed them each a cup swirling with steam. 'Drink this. It will calm your nerves.'

'But the suspicion is quickly spreading, Miriam.' Cosima laid a hand on her arm. 'We think you should leave the city with us at once. None of us is guilty, but our sympathies for the baiting animals could be our undoing. Stourbridge Fair in Cambridge begins next month, and astrological readings are always in great demand. We'll be gone for six weeks. No one will challenge your departure from London if it's for work.'

184

'And abandon my patients, my animals and my garden?' Miriam shook her head after a sip of tea. 'I shall not.'

'But if anyone finds out we fed the baiting animals we could all be strung up,' Isaac replied sombrely. 'A man died. People are calling for justice.'

'Osborne's death is nobody's fault but Osborne's,' Miriam sighed. 'He was a despicable man and, while he may not have deserved to be killed, it's a miracle one of his animals had not despatched him before.' She tenderly patted Cosima's hand. 'Thank you for your concern, my dears, but I can only leave London for a day or two at the most.'

'It's not just the bear and the wildcat animals, is it, Miriam?' Cosima asked softly, reading the worry in the older woman's face. 'Why can't you leave?'

Miriam met Cosima and Isaac's stares. 'I have seen a calamity written in the stars. Something catastrophic is going to happen in London before the autumn equinox at the end of September. I would never forgive myself if I wasn't here to help stop it.'

'That's next month.' Isaac stepped towards her and lay a hand on her forearm. 'What did you see?'

'In July, a comet blazed over London with a swift and smouldering flame unlike any I have seen before. Another once passed over the city foretelling the Plague. But that comet was slower, and it had trudged across the black with a heavy and foreboding pace. This one was different. It blistered the night sky in an explosion of fire.'

'What do you think will happen?' Cosima asked. 'Is it the Dutch? Are they going to attack the city? They say the English navy burned almost an entire town of theirs to the ground. Holland is outraged.'

'I don't know exactly what will occur,' Miriam said, 'but I believe there is a way I can protect the city. A dream has visited me many times, showing me how to prevent disaster. I must ensure six ravens are keeping guard at the Tower of London. I have delivered far more than six there already. Jet regularly checks on his brothers, sisters and cousins, and they keep watch all over the city. They will warn us when the time comes.'

Cosima and Isaac looked at one another gravely as Isaac drew a crumpled piece of paper from his pocket and handed it to Miriam. The title THE VISION OF MARCUS RATHDER, CONCERNING LONDON was printed over a woodcut of several people surrounding fire with geometric shapes hovering above them. 'Rathder has been circulating his own prophecy all over London. He's also claiming that a catastrophe is brewing in the city.'

Miriam examined the prediction and frowned. 'I cannot make sense of this. It's as cryptic as a hieroglyph.' She stared at it, her lips pursing. 'No doubt that was his intention. The more confusing it is, the more open to interpretation it becomes. I wonder what Rathder is up to with this prophecy? He does nothing unless it's for his own gain.'

'People are saying it indicates a fire.' Cosima pointed to the blaze in the middle of the illustration.

Miriam nodded. 'Apocalyptic visions of fire always arise during a drought. London has not seen significant rain for nearly a year. We must all hope for it soon.'

Isaac's brow creased, then his eyes shone with an idea. 'Come with us to the Stourbridge Fair before this mishap strikes. The ravens will know where to find you. You will have defended the city from harm, and by the time we return to London the lost Bartholomew Fair animals would have been found or forgotten about. Not only will you be safe from this threat to London and those who want to blame you for the escaped bear, but your astrological readings in Stourbridge will bring about a financial boon for you! It's the most popular event in the country. You'll have people lining up!'

Miriam smiled. 'That's very shrewd of you, my dear, but Stourbridge is too far for the ravens to fly in an emergency and, as you know, I am fortunate enough not to need money. Your uncle left me enough to carry on his and Culpeper's legacy of treating the poor for free, and the queen has made generous donations to my cause. With regard to the Bartholomew Fair animals –' she turned to Rosie, who was now pressing her head against the peepholes at the back of the fireplace with her tail flicking excitedly – 'it implies guilt for me to abandon my house and garden straight after their departure.'

'But what if the mob comes here to question you?' Isaac added. 'There's no telling how far their wrath will take them.'

'I am not afraid of being accused.' Miriam shrugged. 'Rathder and Moore have already tried to coax me into a confession, and they got nowhere because I honestly had no idea what they were talking about.' She strode to Rosie, who was too absorbed in catching sight of Jet, Asta and Lipa inside the priest hole to notice her approach. 'That was until I found the fugitives hiding in my garden this afternoon.'

Miriam pressed the soot-covered brick with her foot, and Rosie uttered a little shriek of fright. The secret door slid open, and Asta and Lipa flinched and scurried under a table in the centre of the chamber – the tablecloth caught up on the bear cub's rear end and exposed the arch of his back and tail to the room.

'If the mob chooses to waste their time here,' Miriam added, 'my priest hole has a passageway that leads to my boat on the river. The wildcat and the bear cub will be safe within its walls in the meantime.'

'How did they get here?' An incredulous smile drew across Cosima's lips. 'It's wonderful to see them free of the baiting ring, but, Miriam –' the blood drained from her face – 'this incriminates you even if you had nothing to do with their escape.'

Jet fluttered to Miriam's shoulder and his feathers puffed with pleasure as she greeted him with a scratch under his beak. 'Not if I rewild them in a few days, once the alarm from the fair has subsided. I will take them with me on a foraging excursion by boat.' Miriam sipped her camomile infusion. 'I harvest for two days each month according to the moon. A fresh cycle starts at the break of September, and I am organizing my trip as we speak.'

'That's three days away,' Cosima noted.

'The new moon draws out the most powerful medicinal properties in plants and herbs,' Miriam replied, 'and it signifies new beginnings – it will be a fortunate time for the wildcat and the bear cub to embark on their new lives.'

'Where are you taking them?' Isaac glanced at Lipa's backside, still protruding from beneath the tablecloth, and laughed softly.

'Epping Forest via the Hackney Marshes. It's close enough to London if I need to hurry back to the city and it's one of my favourite places to collect hawthorn, dandelion, nettles, fungi, willow, hazelnuts and pine resin. I will deliver our new friends there. It has ample territory for them to make their own.' She looked at the table sombrely. 'I just hope the dense woodland will give them enough protection from humans.'

Cosima and Isaac glanced at one another and shared the same thought.

'We can't let you do this alone,' Cosima said. 'It's too dangerous.'

'We'll help you in any way we can, but we need to act as soon as possible,' Isaac said firmly. 'In three days, the mob may have already pounced, and I don't want to think what will happen to you and these animals if you are caught.'

'Very well, I have been wondering how an old woman like me could handle a bear cub alone, and the added security of being together will benefit us all,' Miriam agreed. 'But only if we have organized ourselves sufficiently and you are both willing to accompany me into the forest. Then no one will question that we are leaving for a foraging expedition.' She clasped her hands together and met Cosima's and Isaac's smiles. 'Let's get to work, my dears. We need to build a box to conceal our new friends for the journey. Come with me. I have plenty of wood and willow branches in the garden, then we shall depart as soon as we are ready.'

Asta swallowed. Three days. She had to rescue Ash from Rathder's house before it was too late. She stood on four paws and winced.

How was she going to rescue Ash when her hind leg could hardly bear her weight?

CHAPTER TWENTY-ONE

RESCUE

Night was falling when claws clacked upon Miriam's cool stone floor, and the bull mastiff and the other dogs trotted into her workshop with their tails wagging triumphantly and their tongues lolling out of their mouths.

'Jasper, Bonny, Bo!' Miriam leaped up from the table, where she, Isaac and Cosima were nursing bowls of Miriam's fresh soup amongst a scattering of wood and willow branches that they were weaving into a box for Lipa and Asta to hide inside for the journey ahead. The dogs crowded around her ankles, nuzzling her calves and jumping on their hind legs. 'I was starting to worry about you!' She stumbled against their weight and greeted them with tender rubs behind their ears and gentle pats upon their flanks. 'I hope Rathder and Moore did not do anything to hurt any of you?' She inspected them and smiled as the dogs wriggled and panted without a scratch on them. 'Come, then.' Miriam stepped to the end of her long table, filled three bowls with cuts of mutton and set them down near the fireplace.

Tucked behind the entrance to the priest hole that Miriam had left ajar, Asta and Lipa watched the dogs wolf the food. They had rested there throughout the day and explored the secret passageway, stretching into a dusty underground tunnel that led to the small dock where Miriam's small sailboat was tied. Miriam's medicinal meat and the smell of the small fire had been comforting, and, although Asta would never admit it, she had felt safe for the first time since she had left the forest. But Lipa was yet to say a word. Where he had once scoffed the rotting food they were given at the Bartholomew Fair, he now merely nibbled his share. Asta refused to leave his side, and the bear cub let out small sighs of sadness every time she leaned her body against his.

The white terrier placed a piece of gristle on the ground. Jet dived from the large oak mantle to his bowl and snatched it in his beak before he swooped into the priest hole.

'Hey!' the white terrier growled. 'Get your own, Jet!'

Jet winked mischievously at the wildcat and the bear

cub. 'The thing is, food always tastes nicer when it's picked off another's plate.'

'You missed a merry broil, my friends.' The bull mastiff yawned, stretching out her front legs before reclining on her stomach beside the small fire. The whippet and the white terrier joined her and licked their chops for a final taste of their meal. 'We chased those men all the way to Rathder's Apothecary Shop in Gunpowder Alley.'

Asta's ears pricked.

'The thin one shrieked almost the whole way there.' The white terrier laughed. 'The bigger one was as scared as a lamb.'

'How I would've loved to chomp his broad backside!' The whippet let out a mock, exaggerated growl, and the three dogs chortled.

'We circled the building all afternoon,' the bull mastiff chuckled. 'Those brutes were trapped inside all day.'

'Did you see a cat like me at the apothecary shop?' Asta asked urgently. 'He often sits at the windowsill that overlooks the small garden at the back of the house. He's my brother.'

The white terrier nodded. 'Yes, he jumped a mile when we neared, and bolted out of sight. The grey cat that was with him taunted us, though – smirking and prancing on the other side of the glass, knowing it was out of our reach.'

'Its pupils dilated with pleasure to see us suffer,' the whippet scoffed.

'That was until I shocked her from the window,' the bull mastiff interrupted. 'But she's a wily thing, and she didn't disappear for long. She soon leaped from the upstairs window and pranced upon the garden wall to insult and hiss and spit at us. When we barked back at her, she tittered at our frustration and cleaned her paws. She's a devil if ever I saw one.'

Asta's jaw hardened, recalling Beauty's manipulative face. 'But what about my brother? Did you see him again?'

'He peered from the upstairs window, hunched, with his ears flat against his head,' the bull mastiff replied. 'He flinched and hissed every time we barked, but he kept his distance and did not join the cat on the wall.'

'How was he?' Asta swallowed.

The bull mastiff's eyes wandered over her. 'He hasn't got the same life in his eyes as you have, my dear. His are haunted and dark with fear.'

A crescent moon shone over London as Asta limped through the priest hole's secret passageway and into the night. She padded forward, her ears and eyes cocking warily

as an easterly wind gusted
against her whiskers. The tide
was high yet at a constant ebb
from the months of no rain,
and a blanket of cracked
mud stretched before
her. The river was quiet,
and Asta breathed
easier seeing the
city was silent
and still with
only Miriam's
small sailboat

bobbing quietly on the water, which lapped gently against the wooden dock ahead.

It was as Asta carefully jumped on to the crisp, muddy riverbank that wings dived fiercely through the black.

Jet appeared on the wall beside her. 'Asta!' the raven scolded. 'Are you mad? London is seething and scouring the streets for an escaped wildcat and a bear cub. If you're seen, all our efforts will be wasted.'

Asta bristled. 'It's the middle of the night. The humans are sleeping. I can't stay here when I know my brother is suffering, and I can take him away from all of this. I have to see him. He needs my help. Wouldn't you do the same for your brothers and sisters if they were held captive in the Tower of London?'

The raven sighed. 'All right, but how do you think you are going to get there on that paw? Can you climb?'

'It's getting better,' Asta lied, avoiding the question. 'I can manage if I move slowly.'

'Then you have no defence. You are useless to Lipa if you are captured. His mother died so—'

'I know why Tilia died,' Asta snapped. A cold, prickly silence followed as she met the raven's stare, her eyes glittering in the darkness. 'If anything happens to me,' she said at last, her voice wavering, 'promise me that you will get him safely back to the wild, then I will not have failed them.'

'That's a promise *you* must keep,' Jet said firmly. 'And, to make sure you fulfil it, I'm coming with you.'

Asta followed the raven and moved as fast as she could through the dense city gloom. Her fur stiffened as the wind blustered through the streets and rattled windows in their frames above shop signs that creaked on their hinges as they rocked back and forth against the gale. No lights illuminated her way as she skittered forward past rats scavenging through weeks of filth that bespattered the ground. She carefully trotted around the densely packed buildings with Jet circling her from above. He croaked whenever a threat appeared, and the wildcat sought shelter when a coach trotted swiftly past, and a boy carrying a lamp escorted a gentleman, stumbling through the darkness after a night of carousing.

They arrived at the back of Rathder's Apothecary Shop and Asta carefully pawed open the small gate in the wall. They crouched low, their eyes lifting to its three pairs of windows that were open wide to the clammy summer night air. Asta's hackles rose, seeing Rathder and Moore move about the candlelit room on the first floor. Rathder was unrolling a large, illustrated scroll of paper and laying it upon a table, and as the men pinned it down with their hands Beauty weaved around Rathder's arms. On the ground floor below them, Ash was curled up upon the same windowsill from which Asta had seen Tilia and Lipa for the first time, caged and forlorn, on their way to the Bartholomew Fair. Only a few weeks had passed since that day, yet it felt like years ago.

Asta's heart swelled as she padded through the gap in the low garden wall with Jet following closely from behind. She inched through Rathder's straggly lavender and rosemary beds, her gaze flicking warily to the first-floor window. Soon, Ash was above her, and her chest fluttered, seeing his flank rise and fall with sleep through the open window.

'Ash,' she whispered, shuffling on her paws, longing to

join him on the windowsill and press her head against his, but there was nothing she could use to climb, and the ache in her rear leg made it impossible to jump. Ash remained unmoved. 'Ash!'

Jet flew upwards, then with a flurry of his wings, he briskly tapped the window with his beak before landing on the neighbouring boundary wall to keep watch, his ebony feathers disappearing into the darkness like a shadow.

'Pssst!' Asta whispered again. 'Down here!'

Ash turned towards her voice, and Asta's chest tightened, seeing his gaunt face peering down at her with tired, jaded eyes. 'Asta?' He squinted into the darkness, poking his head out of the window. 'What are you doing here?'

'Oh, Ash, I've missed you so much.' Asta smiled. 'Quickly – come with me!' she urged. 'I have made new friends that are going to rewild us. We will return to the forest soon!'

Ash yawned widely.

'What are you waiting for?' Asta frowned. 'There is no time to waste – let's go!'

'When are you going to wake up, Asta?' Ash's eyes narrowed. 'Mother deceived us. The wild isn't what you think it is. It's cruel and bloodthirsty. It was only a matter of time before you and I were murdered, or we starved to death. I won't go back there. The human world is safer. It's where we were destined to stay, and we're lucky to have found it.'

'How can you say that?' Asta frowned. 'The human world is a nightmare. They made me fight in the ring at the Bartholomew Fair. You have no idea what it was like,' she said, bowing her head. 'It was a place of torture. The things I saw will be etched on my mind forever.'

She paused, hoping Ash would acknowledge what she had faced and share a word of comfort as he would have done in the forest, but he only glared at her bitterly. She stared into his piercing yellow gaze and tried to understand it. 'It's fear that's trapping you here.'

'Ha!' Ash spat. 'It's not fear that stops me. It's you.'

A chill rippled up Asta's spine. 'What?'

'You and Mother controlled me,' Ash scowled. 'I couldn't think for myself – *be* myself! I didn't hunt the way she wanted; I couldn't play the way you liked. Nothing I did was ever good enough for either of you.'

Asta's mind whirred, recalling the past, and felt a stab of guilt. She remembered his downcast sighs during their unsuccessful hunting trips and his unwillingness to scuffle sometimes, but she'd had no idea he'd felt this way. 'I'm sorry, Ash,' she mewed earnestly. 'I didn't know—'

'You wanted me to fail, so you would look better in

Mother's eyes,' Ash interrupted, fury rippling over his body. 'So *you* would be her favourite!'

'That isn't true.' Asta shook her head. 'Ash, you are my brother – you're my friend, not my rival.'

'Don't lie to me!' Ash growled, contempt curling his lips back around his teeth. 'I won't be your puppet again. We would be parting ways soon and leading solitary lives in the wild, so what difference does it make whether I return to the wild with you or not? We were always fated to follow different paths.' He rose to leave. 'It's time we forgot one another ...'

'I won't!' Asta cried. 'I'm your sister. I love you. I'm trying to help you ...'

'I don't need you to rescue me, Asta!' Ash whirled on her. 'I have a new life here where I am valued. I can take care of myself.'

'You are a wild animal, Ash. You need to be free!'

'You have no idea what I need! Go, Asta. I have nothing more to say to you after what you did to Beauty and my master.'

'*What?*' Asta glowered.

'You mauled my best friend!'

'I never touched that cat!' Asta hissed. '*She's* the one who is lying to you, Ash! Rathder didn't save people from the plague. He poisoned them then stole—'

'You put my master in danger,' Ash interrupted. 'He's lost so much money since you escaped from the Bartholomew Fair; we don't know where our next meal will come from. Animals were put on this earth to serve the humans, Asta. You shouldn't have run away.'

'You are not yourself.' Asta's tail flicked angrily. 'Those are Beauty's words! How could you become a domestic plaything, Ash?'

But Ash was already leaving. 'I'm surviving, Asta,' he said coldly. 'Pretend I never existed. Hurry back to the wild and never look back.' Asta stared at him, open-mouthed. Ash clenched his jaw, his yellow eyes misting. 'I said get out of here, Asta! Now!'

'No!' Asta pleaded, the words rushing from her mouth. 'Ash, please don't go. I can't go back to the wild without you.' But Ash continued shuffling away. '*Please!* Don't leave, Ash. This is your only chance. You have to come with me, or you'll be trapped in the human world forever.'

'So be it.' Ash paused, talking over his shoulder without meeting Asta's gaze. 'Goodbye, Asta.' His voice wavered. 'You are as dead to me as I am to you.'

He hopped out of sight, and Asta stared at the empty windowsill with her blood ringing in her ears.

Jet glided from the high garden wall and landed beside her. 'Are you all right?'

Asta's voice cracked. 'He doesn't want to come with us.'

'I'm sorry.' The raven sighed softly. 'Now we must return to Miriam's.' He gave her a kind, gentle nudge with his beak, and Asta slowly limped out of Rathder's garden beside him. 'You need to rest after everything you've been through. You must save your strength for the journey ahead. Once you're in the wild, you'll—'

But, before Jet could finish, the raven and the wildcat jumped as a shriek came from Rathder's first-floor window.

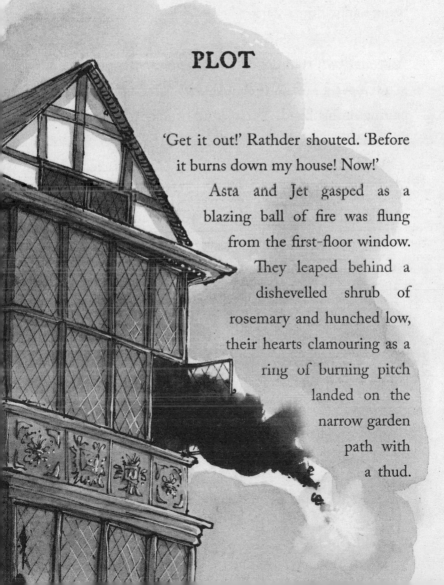

CHAPTER TWENTY-TWO

PLOT

'Get it out!' Rathder shouted. 'Before it burns down my house! Now!'

Asta and Jet gasped as a blazing ball of fire was flung from the first-floor window. They leaped behind a dishevelled shrub of rosemary and hunched low, their hearts clamouring as a ring of burning pitch landed on the narrow garden path with a thud.

Asta's eyes rounded, watching the flames rise and undulate in the wind, and her nose wrinkled as a bitter stench wafted across the gloom. The wildcat and the raven stared up at the window and wished they could hear everything that was being said within.

'You *numskull*!' Rathder barked from above, his arms flailing in a temper, and Beauty fled at once. 'I'm burned!' he cried, puffing on his hand. 'What kind of *idiot* pours aqua vitae on a conflagration?'

'Watch your mouth, you crusty old barnacle,' Moore slurred, swaying as he loomed over Rathder.

Rathder glared into Moore's cold, black eyes. 'Alcohol *incinerates*, you great baboon,' he said through gritted teeth. 'We need a slow and steady pace that will spread efficiently! My experiments prove that pitch and charcoal are the—'

Moore took a swig from a bottle. 'But I want to watch it *burn*!' he cackled. He swerved to the open window and spat a stream of spirit on to the fire below. Its flames whooshed upwards, and Asta and Jet cowered in the rosemary shrub, their eyes glowing in the black against the blaze.

'Stop it, you drunken ass!' Rathder admonished, snatching the bottle from Moore, but Moore was fast and shoved Rathder with his left hand. Rathder stumbled backwards from the force of the blow, and Moore ripped the flask back from Rathder's fist. A moment later, Rathder's backside struck the floorboards, and the pots and bottles clinked around the room.

Moore's face darkened. 'Rathder, you bore me to death.'

Rathder hopped upright with a scowl. 'Then you and your blasted strong water can entertain yourselves elsewhere,' he snapped. 'And take this with you,' he added, thrusting a large canvas sack at Moore's chest. The men glowered at one another. 'The game is afoot. It begins tonight.'

Moore clenched his jaw. 'This better work.'

'Just follow the plan.' Rathder stared back unblinkingly. 'Then once the word is out that my prophecies are accurate, and that Dutch hag has been done away with by the mob – her patients will come crawling back to me. You get our wildcat and that bear cub back, and we'll storm the baiting rings once more. We'll be rich and the money lenders' nooses will no longer hang round our necks.' Rathder spat, his voice rising with resentment. 'We'll loot whatever riches we can find in the panic the fire will bring, but we will make sure the Dutch, the French, the Catholics or the religious or political fanatics are blamed. We'll have vengeance on the city that spurned us!'

Moore grunted his approval. 'And may the Dutch witch

burn in hell.' He stomped away, banging the door behind him.

Instantly, Rathder bent beneath the table. 'Oh, Beauty,' he cooed, lifting the cat into his arms and caressing her. 'You're safe now. That lunatic has gone, my darling girl.' Beauty nestled into his neck. 'Come, let's to bed.' He circled his office and extinguished the candlelit sconces with a pinch of his fingers. 'We have much to do tomorrow.' He lifted a candelabra from the table and exited the room.

Asta and Jet watched as the window above them was plunged into darkness. 'They're up to something,' Asta whispered, daring to pad out from the rosemary bush to stare at the back of Rathder's house, now as silent with sleep as the rest of the street.

A creak sounded. 'Asta! Get back!' Jet gasped.

Asta leaped back under the rosemary shrub just as Moore barged out through Rathder's back door. He galumphed on to the narrow garden path and trod towards the ring of burning pitch with a canvas sack swinging from his shoulder. Asta and Jet held their breaths as his boots stopped just inches from their hiding place. His musky scent of old sweat and tobacco seized the shadows around them as he drew the flask from his pocket, poured a stream of the spirit on to the smouldering fire and chuckled as the flames rose and licked the air. Moore took a generous glug, kicked the pitch into the barren vegetable bed and plodded out of sight, leaving the conflagration to scorch itself out in the dust.

Jet and Asta heaved sighs of relief. 'My heart stopped,' the raven exhaled. 'You're lucky not to have been seen.'

They craned their necks to the upper window above the boundary wall, Asta's ears twitching, hearing the wind howling through the streets and whistle about the timber houses.

'We need to see what they were doing in there,' Asta said.

Jet nodded, stretching out his wings. 'Stay here and keep watch.'

Asta shook her head. 'I'm coming with you.'

'On that leg?' The raven gave Asta a quizzical look, his eyes glinting mischievously.

Asta ignored him. 'Just go.'

Jet took to the air and swooped into Rathder's house a moment later. Asta raced from the rosemary shrub to the boundary wall where an apple tree that had been trained to grow flat against the wall long ago stretched broadly against the bricks. With great effort, Asta climbed it, knocking off small putrefying apples as she went. She moved swiftly, the adrenaline sweeping through her limbs as she hauled herself on to the wall. She trotted to the casement window, her rear paw throbbing. She stepped inside, her heart hammering.

Jet was walking across a round table in the centre of the small room where a large map of London was pinned down by a human skull, a brass plate peppered with dry crusts of bread, a pot of ink with a feather quill sticking out of it and a Church chalice cup – each placed in a corner.

Asta sat on the windowsill and pored over the lines marking a city that blemished fields of open grassland and the snaking shape of the River Thames. It was the first time Asta had seen a map, and, again, she was stupefied and horrified by the capabilities of the human mind.

'We're here –'Jet tapped a small road, labelled *Gunpowder Alley*, with his beak – 'within the walls that were built by the Romans to fortify and define the boundary wall of the city.' The raven continued pecking the paper and stepped from west to east. 'It's two miles long, up to ten feet wide and twenty feet high and surrounds a tangle of medieval streets, lanes and alleys that twist around some of London's oldest timber houses and churches.' Jet stopped, his ebony eyes flicking across the paper. 'Here's Pudding Lane, where we just walked, and that's London Bridge: the only connection to the city and the south side of the river. To the east is Miriam's house and garden, which is close to the Tower of London where my brothers and sisters are keeping watch—'

'Yes, but we know why Rathder and Moore were looking at it, don't we?' Asta interrupted. 'They're going to start a fire.'

'You're right, but when and where it will strike is still a mystery,' Jet went on. 'There's no indication of what they are planning, except what we have just witnessed outside. They have not plotted a route on here. So, by all appearances, this is just an ordinary map. Fires are common in the city, especially in times of drought. The majority of houses are built with timber.' The raven gravely stared into Asta's green eyes, his feathers ruffling in frustration. 'Accidents happen all the time.'

'There must be something here we can use to stop them.' Asta looked about the room. 'If they're plotting to burn London, then my brother is in danger.'

'We all are,' Jet countered, fluttering to a sideboard on the other side of the room that was littered with papers, beakers, flasks, clay pipes and other detritus from Rathder's experiments. Jet flitted about the mess, scraping and clinking porcelain and metal together as he struggled for a firm footing. He put his head inside a bowl and inhaled deeply. 'This is where they have been making pitch – it's highly flammable. Humans harvest it from trees for waterproofing boats, timber houses and buckets. They also use it for making torches they set alight to see in the dark.'

Asta swallowed. 'That's what that ring of fire is made of outside, isn't it?'

'Yes – and it's a shrewd move,' Jet said. 'Pitch is used all over London. It won't trace back to either Rathder or Moore.' Jet trod across a large scattering of papers and turned them over in his beak. 'There's nothing here but recipes and the scribblings of a madman.' He tossed them away from him in a fit of impatience and hopped towards Asta, who was still crouching on the windowsill. 'I need to tell Miriam about this. She's the only one who might be able to—'

It was then that Jet suddenly stumbled through two sheets of paper covering a metal plate that was teetering on the edge of the sideboard. He leaped in a flutter of wings and repositioned himself on a nearby stack of books just as the plate tumbled and smacked against the floorboards below with a tremendous clang. Asta and Jet locked eyes in the darkness as footsteps sounded from within.

'We need something to prove what Rathder and Moore are up to.' The raven frantically searched the sideboard with his beak. 'I don't know if I can make Miriam understand without it.'

'There's no time,' Asta cried, watching a strip of candlelight brightening beneath the door. 'He's coming. Look!' Jet followed her gaze as the door handle rattled. 'We have to go!'

Jet launched upwards, kicking up papers from the sideboard into the air as he went. He soared over Asta, now racing through the window and bounding as fast as she could along the boundary wall to the apple tree. Then, with one last glance over her shoulder to Ash's empty windowsill, she disappeared with the raven into the night.

A second later, Rathder burst through the doorway and glared into the gloom.

'Who's there?' He scowled, the candle he carried flickering as he clumped about the room in his nightshirt, his bare feet treading on a diagram Jet had not seen.

It was of a man hurling pitch on to rooftops.

Below it was another drawing of a crudely drawn cat wearing a strange harness dragging a ring of fire behind it like a plough.

CHAPTER TWENTY-THREE

FIRE

Asta and Jet swerved from Rathder's garden and hurried east. They weaved through the city's alleys, the rising gale gusting about their fur and feathers. Asta thought about Ash with every stride. She had never seen him so ragged and withdrawn. Nor had she heard such anger and resentment in his voice before. She ached for him, knowing how frightened he must have been for all the weeks he'd been alone in the human world, but his words had frightened her. The brother she'd known in the forest had vanished. Beauty had fed off their mother's murder, and shrouded Ash's mind with a darkness that Asta didn't know how to shed. She couldn't imagine returning to the wild without him, but she couldn't get there without Miriam's help, and every minute of delay created a greater danger that they would all be found out. Tilia had already lost her life, and

215

now Miriam was risking hers so that she and Lipa could be free. Yet Asta was sure Ash would perish if she left him behind.

They were halfway back to Miriam's house when Asta spotted a bright orange wisp floating in the air. She slowed as more emerged and heard a clamour of drumbeats and the sharp, rapid clang of church bells pealing in the distance.

'Asta, stop!' Jet croaked, swooping and quickly nudging her behind a discarded crate where a pair of rats fled from a pile of withered cabbage leaves. A second later, a young man sprinted round a corner, followed by an exhausted family in their nightclothes, carrying their belongings in sacks over their shoulders.

The young man hammered a wooden spoon against a metal pot. 'Fire in Pudding Lane!' he cried. 'Wake up! Wake Up! Fire in Pudding Lane!'

'We're too late.' Asta shuddered, staring up at the windows overhead, igniting with the glow of candlelight as the boy passed below. Asta and Jet hunched low as ashen faces peered through the diamonds of glass above.

'Pudding Lane is three streets from here,' Jet whispered. 'Our route back is compromised. The humans will be everywhere.'

'You must go and alert Miriam and Lipa.' Asta turned

towards the way they had already travelled. 'I have to go back and warn Ash.'

'No, Asta.' Jet hopped forward, stretching out his wings and blocking her path. 'He is in league with Rathder and Beauty now. You will be recaptured.'

'I have to do something!' Asta shook her head. 'What if Ash—'

'All we can do now is make a run for it before these roads start swarming with humans,' Jet countered, his eyes roving wildly about the street as men, women, and children stepped from their houses with bundles of their possessions, the gale whirling around their nightshirts and blowing their hats off their heads. 'If Rathder and Moore are behind this, Ash is probably safe.'

Asta considered this, her fur prickling with unease.

'Miriam will know what to do, and Pudding Lane is the most direct route back to her. It's a two-minute dash from end to end – you can do it – the humans will be distracted by the fire.'

'I can't.' Asta stared at the people filling the road ahead, her brow furrowing with dread. 'There will be too many of them.'

'You escaped the Bartholomew Fair, Asta. You can do anything if you believe you can,' Jet reassured, and Asta felt stronger. 'I'll be with you. Stick to the shadows, take cover under whatever you can and don't stop long enough for anyone to realize what you are.'

Asta nodded hesitantly.

'Now, go!' Jet urged, hopping forward and bulking out his wings with Asta padding behind. 'Go!'

Asta's heart pounded as she hobbled as fast as she could through the streets, now crowding with humans either fleeing the conflagration or pointing at the sparks floating on the wind and settling upon the gutters and gables of the houses. She felt the fire before she saw it, her breath smarting as the gale gusted smoke towards her. She turned on to Pudding Lane with a cough, and her chest burned as the heat and the sour smell of smouldering wood, daub, straw, textiles, tar, pitch and countless human chattels were devoured by flames that stretched above the rooftops and illuminated the road in a hellish glow.

Both sides of Pudding Lane were ablaze. The old timber jettied houses were packed so closely together that every speck of fire travelling on the wind spread the inferno through any cracks in the wood or roof tiles it touched. The drought and the long, hot summer had turned the city into a tinderbox, and Asta stared wide-eyed at the people below, urgently filling leather buckets, chamber pots and earthenware bowls from dug out holes in the cobbles on the ground. They hurled underground pipe water on to the houses, and the flames stubbornly billowed and rose seeming to cackle in the rising gale.

'Asta!' Jet dived and prodded her with his beak, but she remained rooted to the spot, transfixed by the fire. 'Come on!'

Asta limped forward and cowered as the roaring fire bellowed over sounds of cracking wood and glass and screaming humans, racing across her path. Some moved in small groups, carrying long cyclinders between their shoulders and spurted water into the blaze, but nothing could tame the flames. The two-minute dash to the end of the road felt never-ending, and relief swept through Asta when she turned on to Lower Thames Street and gulped the fresher air as she left Pudding Lane behind her and hurried east into the wind.

Asta and Jet entered Miriam's house through the priest hole and found Lipa safely where Asta had left him, slumbering beneath the table in Miriam's secret office. Asta pressed her head against his, and the bear cub woke with a start.

'It's all right,' she hushed. 'It's me.'

'Oh, Asta.' Lipa nuzzled her. 'I was frightened you wouldn't come back.' He looked past her, his gaze eagerly combing the gloom. 'Where is your brother?'

'He wouldn't come with us.' Asta's whiskers drooped and the bear cub nestled softly into her neck.

'Stay here.' Jet fluttered to a cord dangling in the darkness and tugged it with beak. 'I'll go to Miriam.'

The concealed door to the kitchen fireplace opened and roused the dogs, stretched out together around the last cinders of the fire, with three sleepy snorts.

'I can smell fear on you, Asta,' the bull mastiff muttered with a sniff. 'What's going on?'

The dogs' ears pricked as Asta recounted what happened. '. . . But we were too late,' Asta concluded. 'A fire has already started on Pudding Lane.'

The dogs scurried to the window, ducked behind the thick curtains and leaped up on their paws, their tails protruding from the fabric.

'Can you see it?' the white terrier yapped, jumping on his hind legs, but he was still too small to peer through the glass.

The whippet nodded. 'There's a glow to the west.'

'And church spires are aflame,' the bull mastiff added gravely.

'Get down, you rogues!' Miriam scolded, hurrying to them by the light of a candelabra she held before her, her long greying hair plait swinging against her white nightshirt. She drew the curtains and swallowed. 'And so it begins.'

'Rathder!' Jet cawed, fluttering to the sill. 'Rathder! Fire! Pudding Lane!'

'It's the catastrophe Rathder foresaw,' Cosima gasped, stepping into the kitchen in her bedclothes with Rosie on her shoulder and Isaac by her side. They joined Miriam at the window; their faces pale as they gazed at the orange haze above the city.

'It is a mishap eventuality foresaw,' Miriam corrected. 'The drought, the wind, and some of the city's oldest wooden houses packed together.' She circled the room and ignited the sconces. 'Let us hope it is swiftly contained and does not spell disaster.'

'Rathder!' Jet squawked again. 'Fire! Apothecary shop!'

'Hush, my love. I heard you the first time,' Miriam said.

'Rathder! Rathder! Rathder!' the raven cried, flapping to her and landing on her long table with a shriek. 'Wildcat! Fire! Rathder!'

'He's gone mad,' Isaac said. Rosie and Cosima were equally perturbed.

'Good grief, Jet,' Miriam said, flinching. 'What has got into you?'

'Rathder! Apothecary shop! Fire! Wildcat! Map! Plot!'

'*Plot?*' Isaac repeated over the din. 'Is Mad Rathder capable of such a thing?'

Miriam paused. 'Perhaps –' she bit her lip with worry – 'with Moore's help.' She returned to the window and stared out at the trees blustering in her garden. 'The wind is blowing from the east, spreading the fire through the city to the west. We still have time to stow valuables and finish our preparations for the bear cub and the wildcat.'

'It won't take us much longer to finish their box.' Isaac went to the table with Cosima, where a timber skeleton of a chest was half woven with willow branches.

'And I must gather my travelling goods.' Miriam hurried to her shelves, collected two wicker baskets, and started filling them with cloth sacks and empty glass jars.

'Rathder! Plot! Stop!' Jet went on, hopping up and down on the windowsill.

'If Rathder is behind this,' Miriam whirled on the raven, 'the fire is already playing out. I will not risk missing my chance to free the bear as I did all those years ago. I won't repeat the same mistake, take time for granted and tempt disaster. My John and the bears would still be with us if I hadn't failed.' Her voice wavered and she paused to collect herself with a deep, calming breath. 'If the fire gets out of control and the wind changes direction, it will come this way and our efforts may be thwarted. The wildcat and the bear cub will be freed, if it's the last thing I do.'

'Rathder! Wildcat! Rath—'

'Shhhh,' Miriam soothed, walking swiftly to the raven and stroking Jet's back feathers. 'All right. I will go to his apothecary shop when everything is prepared. I will find the other wildcat and rescue it.' She scratched under his beak and the raven's shaggy throat feathers puffed with comfort. Miriam looked out at the fiery glow in the city beyond. 'We must hurry.' She closed the curtains and turned to Cosima and Isaac, frenetically weaving the willow branches around Lipa and Asta's box and shooing Rosie away as she chattered and mischievously nibbled at the ends. 'Now, I must get to work.'

Jet fluttered to Asta, staring out from the priest hole with her ears pricked.

She met his gaze and whispered. 'I'm going too.'

Jet shook his head. 'Absolutely not. If you're seen . . .'

'Like you said in Pudding Lane, the humans will be more concerned with the fire than with an escaped wildcat,' Asta said. 'I am going back for my brother, just as you would.'

'I mean it, Asta,' he said firmly. 'If you come with us, you risk all our lives. You must trust me and stay exactly where you are.'

Asta stalked into the priest hole with an angry flick of her tail. Lipa followed and curled up beside her.

A breath of wind travelled up the tunnel and brushed lightly against Asta's fur. She lifted her head and felt the breeze tickle her whiskers.

No one could stop her from following Miriam and Jet once they had left.

Outside in the gloom of Miriam's garden, Moore stepped from behind the trunk of a tree and scuttled across the dry grass, his eyes flicking to the drawn curtains in Miriam's kitchen workshop.

He circled the house, the canvas sack swinging on his shoulder as he seized fistfuls of pitch and cast them beneath the border of leafy geraniums growing around the timber building.

'Now, when the fire reaches you, the flames will burn so brightly, the devil will collect you himself. You will hinder us no more, witch.'

He turned away and disappeared into the night.

CHAPTER TWENTY-FOUR

SUPSECT

Church bells rang across the City of London under a murky swirl of smoke that obscured the scorching midday sun. Miriam strode briskly into the howling gale towards Gunpowder Alley with Jet tightly gripping her shoulder. Asta followed her from a distance, her heart thumping as she trotted against a sea of people, their faces black with soot as they carried everything they owned in bundles that swung from their fists. Some clasped them tightly to their chests while others trundled through the congested street, riding on carts overflowing with more refugees and their salvaged belongings. To Asta's relief, none gave her more than a glance and she swallowed, hoping for that to remain.

'Turn back, madam!' a cart driver cried to Miriam in a thick country drawl. 'You are walking into the mouth of hell! There's room for you on my wagon – it's the finest in all of Kent! Just forty pounds to Moorfields.'

'*Forty pounds!*' Miriam's eyes bulged. 'It should be two shillings!'

'That was before the Almighty unleashed his wrath upon the gluttons in Pudding Lane!' the man cackled, his dry lips drawing back from crooked grey and yellow teeth. Miriam marched on with a disgusted shake of her head. The cart driver swivelled in his seat as he watched her leave, 'All right! Thirty-five pounds, seein' as you don't have any items on your person,' he haggled. Miriam uttered a *tsk* of disapproval. 'And you won't find a better price elsewhere!'

'It's Miriam!' a little girl cried ahead, letting go of her mother's hand to wave.

Miriam smiled without slowing. 'Hello, my dear, I hope that stomach of yours is—'

'Don't talk to her,' her father chided, pulling his daughter close to him. 'She's Dutch! They started the fire. Their spies are everywhere.'

Heads snapped in Miriam's direction, their eyes round with alarm. Miriam quickened, her shoulders drooping with hurt.

The little girl peeked back at her with a confused frown. 'My feet ache, Father,' she moaned as her parents hurried her away. 'Why can't we take a boat or a cart like we normally do?'

'It's too expensive,' her mother replied, stealing an anxious glance at Miriam. 'Come along. Moorfields is not much further.'

Asta followed Miriam and Jet as they slipped into a lane to the right and headed north, hoping to bypass the fire marauding to the west. The further they travelled, the more deserted the city became, and soon the ground beneath them began to warm and a hot blizzard of ash whirled about them, coating them in white, powdery flecks like snow.

Round the next corner, they were swallowed by a dense cloud of smoke, and Miriam guided herself forward, tracing the buildings on the side of the road with her fingertips. Asta hurried, worried she would lose them, and, knowing she was safely cloaked by the smoke, she hovered at Miriam's heels. She craned her neck for the shop signs creaking above her head in the gale, but she saw nothing but a blanket of grey.

'I can't see, Jet.' Miriam coughed, standing still and squinting in the smoke. The raven clucked and warily darted his head about in the blur.

Asta's breath halted, hearing the brisk pitter-patter

of rushing footsteps sound on the cobbles and quickly grow louder with every beat of her thumping heart. A second later, they gasped as a figure burst through the haze. Miriam cried out as their shoulders struck, and a young man cursed as the bag in his grasp spilled plates, jewellery, brass candlesticks and silver cutlery that jingled and clanged as they tumbled upon the ground. He swiftly scooped them back into his arms and vanished.

They froze.

'Looters,' Miriam whispered, steadying herself with a stroke of the raven's feathers.

'Careful!' Jet croaked. 'Careful!'

They shuffled on, the ground getting hotter and hotter the further west they dared to tread. Before long, sparks glittered, and a distant roar of fire rumbled like thunder over screams ahead.

They turned on to Gunpowder Alley and could travel no further against a blistering wall of heat. 'We're too late.' Miriam covered her mouth against the smoke. Asta's eyes stung, just able to make out furious orange flames licking black skeletons of houses on the street ahead. 'Rathder's Apothecary Shop is no more.'

'It's over!' a man shouted somewhere in the white.

'There's nothing to be done!' another added. 'To Moorfields!'

'It's gone!' a voice Asta recognized wailed somewhere behind her. 'Everything I have is *gone*!'

Miriam blindly stepped backwards and bumped into something bony and waxy. Asta whirled round with a jolt of alarm. A white face with circular glass eyes and a long beak loomed at Miriam in the smoke.

'Miriam!' it growled.

Miriam glared. 'Marcus Rathder?' She replied, her gaze narrowing. 'Robbing from the afflicted even in times of calamity, I see?' She glanced to the right, sensing a presence over her shoulder.

Moore stood behind her, shoving a silver candlestick into the same sack he had carried on his shoulder the previous night. 'Dutch hag.'

'Where is the wildcat you have been keeping in your apothecary shop?' Miriam turned to Rathder. Asta's hackles rose. 'I'll pay you enough money for a boat and a cart out of the city, and I will tell no one of your thieving.'

'My apothecary shop is gone!' Rathder tugged at the leather hat upon his head in despair. 'I have lost *everything*! I have nothing but the clothes on my back and this plague suit I wore to tend to the afflicted today—'

'And yet you foresaw this disaster?' Miriam said with a wry frown.

'I saw a vision of an inferno! I knew fire would come, just like everybody did! I was not the only one! I never thought it would take everything from me!' he howled, his volume increasing hysterically as running footsteps approached through the smoke. 'My livelihood! My cats! Everything I had is gone!'

Miriam stared at the flames. 'Your cats were *inside*?'

Asta looked into the fire and felt the blood drain from her body. How could Ash be gone when they had talked just the night before? She quailed, summoning her last moments with him. If she had said the right things, he would be with them now. She'd never forgive herself for not forcing him to come with her. A bitter stab of grief lurched in her. Her failure to convince him to leave had killed him.

At that moment, a burly man appeared through the smoke with two other men, clutching clubs in their fists. 'There's no use standin' here and watchin' this mess when you can do somethin' to stop it!' he urged, and the men beside him nodded their heads. 'They're tearin' down the houses with fire hooks. Even the king himself is tacklin' the blaze, but there's no stoppin' it! It's croppin' up all over the city – even in places beyond the conflagration! There's no sense to it! There's a plot afoot, I tell you – it's Dutch retribution!'

'It's the French!' a thin man scoffed beside him.

'It's the Catholics!' the third man blared.

'It was *her* people.' Moore grabbed Miriam's forearm, and Jet flapped in alarm. Asta hissed, but nobody heard it. The men closed in on her and she struggled in Moore's grasp. 'She's Dutch! And she is harbouring an Italian acrobat – a *Catholic* – in her house!'

'She's carrying fireballs!' Rathder added. 'I saw her cast them into the houses!'

'Lies!' Miriam cried, trying to wriggle free of Moore's hold. 'Get your hands off me!'

'She's a rebel of the highest degree!' Moore yelled. 'She protested at the Bear Gardens, and she orchestrated the stampede at the Bartholomew Fair! She hates this city – she wants it to burn!'

'So *you* started the fire!' the burly man spat, leering over her, his fingers tightening on the club in his hand.

Jet shrieked. In a flash of ebony, he burst upon Moore and dug his talons into his chin. With a scream, Moore stumbled backwards, withdrawing his hand from Miriam and shooting it towards Jet. He snatched the raven by the neck and pummelled him, trying to stop Jet gusting about his face and pecking his nose and cheeks, with his other fist.

'Stop it!' Miriam cried, her voice shrill with panic as she thwacked him, but Moore was unmoved. 'Let go of him!'

A ferocious snarl erupted from Asta's throat, and she rocketed through the smoke and raked her claws across Moore's cheek.

'A devil!' one of the men gasped as Moore threw Jet from him.

'No!' Rathder growled. 'That's my wildcat this hag stole from the Bartholomew Fair!'

'After her!' Moore bellowed.

'Run!' Jet croaked, launching unsteadily into the air.

Asta and Miriam sprinted into the smoke with heavy strides stomping after them.

Miriam's front door flew open and struck a wall with a bang, making Lipa, Isaac, Cosima, Rosie and the three dogs jolt in alarm. The dogs' barks silenced a moment later as Miriam and Asta raced into the room. They were covered in ash and carried with them the cloying, acrid smell of smoke.

'How are our preparations?' Miriam asked breathlessly, cradling Jet in her arms. Asta leaped back inside the priest hole and curled up against Lipa.

'It's done.' Isaac went to her with Cosima, their brows creasing with worry. 'The box for the wildcat and the bear cub is finished and on the boat, along with your belongings and the chickens. Your valuables are safely buried in the garden.'

'Thank you.' Miriam placed Jet on the large table in the middle of the room and tenderly inspected him for injuries. Her face was black with soot and her cheeks were streaked with tears. Asta's and Lipa's ears flattened, watching the raven tremble a little on his talons. A small sob escaped Miriam's lips as she embraced him with a deep sigh of relief. 'We must leave immediately –' she brushed away her tears – 'before the wind changes and blows the fire this way.'

Cosima nodded. 'I'll help you get the last of your things.'

'What happened?' Isaac asked as Miriam filled two bowls with a pitcher of water and placed one in front of Jet then Asta. Both slurped it at once. She poured more water into the cup of her hand and vigorously washed the soot from her face.

'The fire is ravaging the city.' Miriam lifted the jug to her mouth and gulped hungrily before catching her breath and setting it down. 'I've never seen anything like it – it's like Armageddon. Swarms of people are escaping through the streets, and looters are everywhere.'

'Did you find Rathder?' Isaac asked, hurrying around the room with them and filling a wicker basket with Miriam's pestle and mortar.

'I saw him, and that dastardly Moore too, filling his arms with swag,' Miriam replied, swiftly picking small bottles of her most cherished remedies from her shelves and filling her deep skirt pockets with precious vials. 'Rathder's Apothecary Shop was consumed by the fire. He was raving hysterically, claiming that he had lost everything to the flames –' she paused and sighed sadly – 'including his cats.'

All the animals in the room stared sadly at Asta. Lipa drew Asta closer to him and she buried her face in his fur, feeling that the throb of grief might swallow her whole.

'Would Rathder sacrifice all he has to prove his prophecy?' Isaac questioned.

'God only knows,' Miriam replied. 'The world has gone mad.' She scanned the room a final time. 'I never want to see him or Moore again. They attacked us. If it wasn't for this wildcat, I'm not sure we would have made it back.'

'She followed you?' Cosima baulked with Isaac. Jet glanced at the priest hole and smiled softly with gratitude. Lipa gave Asta a gentle nudge of pride.

'Thank goodness she did. Now, for heaven's sake, let's go. There are men prowling the streets with clubs and blaming foreigners for the conflagration.'

'What do you mean "foreigners"?' Cosima frowned.

'Anyone they see fit,' Miriam answered, rousing the dogs with brisk claps of her hands. 'Me for being Dutch, you for being a Catholic. Now, let's round up the animals and get out of here.'

Jet flew to the priest hole. 'Ready?' he asked Asta and Lipa. They nodded, both rigid with nerves. 'Follow me.'

They were crossing the kitchen workshop and heading towards Miriam's back garden door when Isaac halted. 'Wait!' he said, grabbing Miriam and Cosima and forcing them to stand still. The three of them listened, wide-eyed. The animals' hackles rose, hearing the same sound.

'Is it the fire?' Cosima gasped.

Miriam shook her head. 'It's the mob.'

CHAPTER TWENTY-FIVE

THE MOB

The clamour outside rapidly grew louder, and Miriam drew a sharp breath of dread. 'Isaac, bolt the back door. I'll lock the front, and Cosima –' she shouted over her shoulder as she raced into the corridor – 'close the curtains and get the animals into the priest hole!'

Everyone leaped into action as the sound of people shouting *'Dutch hag! Dutch hag! Dutch hag!'* rose every second. Asta and Lipa were the first inside the priest hole, followed by the dogs and Cosima and Rosie, clinging to her chest.

Fists pounded on the back and front doors, and the dogs barked.

'Miriam!' Rathder's voice cried over the horde encircling the house. 'We followed you here, and we saw that Catholic wench draw the curtains! We know you're in there! Get out now before we burn your house to the ground!'

There was a scuffle of feet.

'Hurry!' Cosima cried as Miriam then Isaac reappeared.

Miriam pushed her nephew into the priest hole before she leaped in after him. She pulled the cord dangling from the wall and sealed them inside.

The pack of scowling Londoners jeered as Rathder bellowed through the bolted front door with his plague suit billowing in the gale. Moore looked on, his eyes bright with malevolence.

'Miriam!' Rathder cried again. 'This is your last chance! Come out now, or justice will be paid!'

'She's not scared enough,' Moore sneered. 'She'll hide in there until we smoke her and her animals out. Our wildcat and the bear cub will be among them, you'll see. Then we can leave her to the flames.'

Rathder stepped away from the door. 'So be it.'

Moore pulled a knife and a rock of flint from his pocket. He knelt to the ground and struck them together against the border of long grasses growing around the house. A spark flashed, and an ember sprung. Moore cupped his hand round where it lay and puffed and blew. A second later, it ignited.

'An eye for an eye, a tooth for a tooth, Miriam!' Rathder yelled. 'You destroy our livelihoods – we take yours too.'

'*An eye for an eye, a tooth for a tooth!*' the mob echoed, their chants growing louder as they watched the fire rise in the wind and race across the old timber building. '*An eye for an eye, a tooth for a tooth! An eye for an eye, a tooth for a tooth!*'

Smoke plumed, wood and glass cracked and the mob staggered backwards from the heat of the fire.

Moore turned to Rathder. 'Get the cats and finish the spread through the city,' he whispered, grimacing at the burning building. 'I will dispose of Miriam and bring our wildcat and the bear cub to our meeting place as planned.'

Rathder nodded and cried out to the mob, his bony finger pointing towards the beleaguered city crumbling in the inferno behind them, 'Now follow me! We must stop the invaders destroying our streets!'

The mob blared and shook self-righteous fists in the air. Rathder led them away, leaving Moore in the garden alone, savouring the flames devouring Miriam's home. His dark eyes gleamed with the flicker of the blaze. He scanned the windows and tightened his grip on the club in his hand, waiting for her and her animals to flee.

Minutes passed, and a scowl deepened across Moore's brow. He strode to the building, his face reddening in the heat as he bent to the crackling fire and listened for cries, for barking, for panicking voices, yet there was none. He quickened his pace and peered into window after window, but he saw no one within.

With a yell of anger, he snapped his head to where the trees blustered around Miriam's garden-wall gate, leading to her private dock and the river beyond.

Asta raced after Jet and bounded from the priest hole with Lipa at her heels and Miriam, Cosima, Rosie, Isaac and the dogs closely following. They hurried across the jetty over the cracked, muddy shore, their heads darting warily from left to right. London Bridge was alight and the river was crowded with floating discarded furniture and boats rowing people and their meagre belongings downstream. Many held their faces in their hands while others gazed back at the hellish tempest of fire rumbling like thunder as the flames gorged on the tightly packed houses and the church spires.

'Everyone keep close to the bear cub,' Miriam urged, pulling the bullmastiff towards Lipa. 'And pray he will look like another dog from afar.'

Isaac and Cosima crowded around him, and together they successfully shielded him from view. They clambered down the stairs to the boat, with Isaac creeping forward, taking Miriam and Cosima's bags and baskets and lifting the hatch that led to the boat's modest lower quarters that he and Cosima had spent the day neatly packing with boxes. The chickens clucked in surprise as light poured in, and Isaac placed the last of their belongings inside. He lifted the large willow box he and Cosima had crafted overnight and stood it on the stern. He swung open its double doors. 'Come on,' he said softly, turning to Asta and Lipa and clicking his tongue.

Asta and Lipa paused on the steps with their ears flicking.

'I don't want to be caged again, Asta,' Lipa said under his breath.

'Nor do I.' Asta swallowed. 'But this is our only way back to the wild.'

She reluctantly padded forward with Lipa edging after her, and Isaac slid a thin branch across the doors and closed them inside. The box was snug yet roomy enough for both of them when they were curled up together. Air flowed freely through the gaps in the weave and, while few would think to peer in, they could see out. They watched Miriam, Cosima, Rosie and the dogs step onboard and gasped as the boat lurched under their shifting weight.

Rosie clambered on top of the box, and Jet fluttered beside her. 'Try not to worry,' the raven reassured. Asta and Lipa stared up at him, unconvinced, 'Remember – you'll feel the forest beneath your paws soon.'

'Untie the mooring rope!' Miriam cried, unravelling the sail billowing wildly in the wind. Cosima leaped up and joined the battle to fasten it into place.

It was as Isaac jumped back on to the jetty and bent over the mooring hook when heavy footsteps sprinted towards him from above.

'Danger!' Jet shrieked. 'Danger!'

But it was too late.

With a tremendous shout, Moore threw himself into Isaac. They crashed into the belly of the boat, and Miriam, Cosima, Rosie and Jet cried out in alarm, stumbling as the boat rocked precariously from side to side against the force of the blow. Jet stormed into the air and dived towards Moore, flapping around his ears, but the raven's attacks spurred Moore's frenzy. The dogs rushed at him, and Asta and Lipa cowered inside the willow box as he kicked the dogs away and struck Isaac with his fists. The bullmastiff flew at him, but Moore was fast and countered the charge with a great barge of his shoulder. The bullmastiff hurtled backwards and hit her head on the side of the boat. She lay there, unmoving. The whippet shivered and hung back, and the white terrier yapped, not daring to confront Moore alone.

'Isaac!' Cosima yelled, hurling herself upon Moore. But her petite frame was like that of a child's, and Moore tossed her from him like a doll before a dull thud sounded, and Isaac fell limp against the boards with a groan. Cosima whimpered and hurried to him on her hands and knees. She embraced him with trembling arms. Rosie bounded to them and hopped up and down, squeaking and chattering with worry.

'Miriam!' Moore growled, stalking towards her. She stared at him from the bow of the boat, holding a boat hook across her chest. Jet fluttered to her shoulder with a caw of warning, and Moore's face contorted with rage. 'You and your tricks are finished.'

'Get off my boat.' Miriam's fingers trembled and tightened round the hook.

Moore threw his head back, and a cold, sinister laugh erupted from his throat. A deadly silence followed as his black eyes landed on Miriam once more.

A second later, he pounced, and Asta and Lipa shuddered as Miriam swiped the hook. Moore took the blow on his forearm and ripped it free from her with his other hand. He shoved her backwards, and she landed heavily on the bow of the boat with a gasp. Jet rocketed upwards and dived again at Moore, but Moore batted the hook and clipped the raven in the flank, hurling him downwards, and he crash-landed beside Isaac at the stern of the boat with a squawk of pain.

Asta's lips pulled back from her teeth, and Lipa stiffened with fury, scenting the stench of the man who had killed his mother. Their eyes met, and with vicious growls rising in them, the wild swept through them. With bitter snarls, the wildcat and the bear cub summoned all the grief and fear and desperation that had haunted them in the human world and burst from the box.

Moore felt the burn of claws raking down his back and let out a squeal of horror. He spun round unsteadily, whipping the boat hook through the air. Asta ducked, and Lipa swerved, just dodging the clout.

Moore's eyes flitted between the wildcat and the bear cub. 'I knew it!' he spat, his gaze widening. He staggered upright and lurched towards Miriam with the boat hook lifted over his head like an axe.

A second later, Lipa hurtled into his gut, and Moore tumbled overboard with a petrified howl. Miriam yanked the sail until it caught the wind, and the gale blasted the boat down the river.

Drifting on the current behind them, Moore
gulped and struggled, then sank into the swirl
of brown water, never to be seen again.

CHAPTER TWENTY-SIX

THE LION'S DEN

'Cosima, grab the rudder!' Miriam cried, racing to the stern of the boat. Cosima looked up with tears running down her cheeks. 'Quickly, my dear, before another disaster befalls us.'

Cosima did as she said, and Miriam took her place, crouching before Jet, Isaac and the bullmastiff. She tenderly lay her hands on all of them, and the raven clacked softly as he slowly stood on his talons and shook his feathers. Miriam pulled a vial from her skirt pocket and waved it under Isaac and the bullmastiff's nose. They roused, their eyes snapping open. The whippet and the white terrier crowded around the bullmastiff with wagging tails, and as they covered her with licks as she leaned and reclined upright with her tongue lolling out of her mouth.

'Here,' Miriam said softly, helping Isaac sit up. He winced. She drew out a larger flask and handed it to him.

He sipped, and coughed a moment later. 'That would cripple a giant!'

'My apple cider is the best remedy for a fright.' She twinkled, slumping beside him and taking a glug of it herself, heaving a deep sigh of relief before handing it to Cosima. She swigged it and spluttered.

Miriam stared at Asta and Lipa, hunching beside the willow box and shook her head in disbelief. 'How could humans think they could lord over you?'

Asta and Lipa met her gaze, and Miriam smiled softly as they looked away.

Everyone sat in silence and shuddered, watching the churches, the shops, the workshops, and the warehouses succumb to the fire. Beneath them, countless cellars storing everything from books, paper, brandy, pitch, resin, tar, brimstone, wax, tallow, sugar, brandy, cotton, silk, coal, gunpowder and timber, fuelled the spread. St Paul's Cathedral towered above the smouldering rooftops. Its timber scaffolding was alight, and centuries of wood, stone, dust and cobwebs fed the inferno within. The flames stretched into the sky and grazed a gargantuan black cloud, stretching fifty miles to the west downwind, that glittered with sparks circling on the gale and spread embers across the tightly packed houses silhouetted against the blaze.

Asta stared at the thousands of incandescent windows, and a lump swelled in her throat. Somewhere, Ash had perished in the flames. She thought of how terrified he must have been, and her eyes flooded with tears. If she had said or done something differently, he would be returning to the wild with her and Lipa now.

'It's like the end of the world.' Cosima shook her head, and Miriam and Isaac nodded sombrely, watching throngs of people flee on foot along the riverbank. Women wearing fine dresses and men wearing periwigs queued to board rowboats. The rest of the crowd plodded east. Some carried heavy loads on their heads. Others had nothing but the clothes on their backs.

'Aunt!' Isaac abruptly sat taller and pointed downstream.

Miriam stared at the river beyond. 'Quickly,' she said, hurrying to the mainsail and slowing the boat. 'Get the wildcat and the bear cub back in the box. Isaac, grab an oar,' she said, and he joined her, carefully manoeuvring an oar into the oarlock. They grunted as they pulled the boat through the water. 'If we're swift, we might get through before it gets too congested.'

Asta and Lipa turned, and their ears flattened. A cluster of vessels and discarded furniture jammed the water ahead as boatmen gathered to stare at the conflagration. The wildcat and the bear cub scrambled into the willow box, and Cosima closed the doors behind them.

'Stay still and stay quiet,' Rosie whispered, nervously tightening her black tail round Cosima's neck.

'Shhhhhh,' Jet hushed, landing on the top of the box. 'We are entering the lions' den.'

Asta and Lipa hardly dared breathe as the sound of chatter soon surrounded Miriam's boat. Boatmen with sun-creased skin and sweat dampening their clothes and hair bobbed beside them.

There was a clunk as Isaac's oar thumped against another boat.

'OI!' a heavy-set boatman cried, and his passengers scowled in Isaac's direction. 'Watch it, pretty boy!'

'Don't draw attention to us,' Miriam said under her breath, retracting her oar, and Isaac did the same. 'We cannot pass. We must wait for the jam to clear.'

The boat slowed and drifted on the water into the middle of the crush that reached all the way to the shore, where more people were clambering into boats from the low river wall. A shiver crawled over Asta as she and Lipa scented the crowd and listened to the boatmen gossip over the rhythmic slap of water striking the hulls of the boats.

'The king's barge has been up and down these waters,

and now the king and his brother have ordered houses to be pulled down to create fire breaks that will stop the spread.' The boatman nodded east where some toppled houses had disappeared from view among the distant sea of tiled roofs, sending puffs of dust into the air. 'The king's brother and his firefighters will stop at nothing to quench the fire!'

'They're too late!' another boatman scoffed. 'The fire is moving too fast for their efforts to work. Foreigners are starting fires all over the city.'

Cosima shared an anxious glance with Isaac and Miriam, and hung her head.

'I heard the Dutch and the French were responsible – this is an act of war!'

'They are skulking through the streets with fireballs and grenades in their pockets! London is burning at the hands of outlanders!'

'The city was already festering with them. Now they have brought London to its knees.'

'I heard there's a rich Dutch woman to the east of the city who is a spy.'

Isaac's jaw hardened. 'I've had enough of this,' he growled, moving to stand.

'Don't!' Miriam hushed. 'I hate it too, but there is too much at stake. If a confrontation turns nasty and the bear cub and wildcat are found, we are finished.' Isaac looked at Cosima. She shook her head despairingly, and he crossed his arms with a frustrated sigh.

'Where is the rain?' a passenger yelled, shaking his fist at the cloudless sky above. 'It's the only thing that will save us!'

'That's because this fire is an act of God!' his wife cried, covering her face with her hands. 'We are being punished for our sins! It started on Pudding Lane – the hub of gluttony.'

'It is not only gluttony,' a bejewelled woman wearing a velvet hat added. 'It is the year 1666. Remember the Book of Revelations? The number of Satan is six-six-six! In one year, we have had plague, war and hellfire. We live in a profane and ungrateful city that is ruled by a proud and lustful court. We must repent!'

'Look at the sun!' her husband gasped. Everyone on the water stared into the sky at an ominous red disc burning behind a veil of smoke. 'It's like an eye staring down with rage at the city.'

'Nonsense.' A nearby boatman rolled his eyes. 'God already punished us with the Great Plague. It was an accident waiting to happen. Our old city is made of wood and is lit by candles and fireplaces – fires are common! It's the drought and the wind that brought this on – no war, no act of God.'

'Don't be so harebrained!' another boatman said, leaning forward with a conspiratorial smirk. 'Think where the fire started: in a bakery, with ovens full of wood and flour just waiting to go up in smoke, and in a part of the city where the streets are the narrowest and most stuffed together – and all of them were old and constructed from timber. The fire was started in the dead of night, on the quietest day of the week when the tide was low, and no water could be reached to extinguish the flames. It was a sinister plot.'

'Look!' the bejewelled woman shrieked. 'Up there!' she whimpered, pointing towards an old church's squat bell tower. 'A devil is spreading the fire!'

The people turned. A figure cloaked in black, wearing a white, long-beaked mask, briefly emerged from behind a nearby chimney breast, tugging a cat by a chain fixed to the collar round its neck, and dragged it from the other side of the rooftop. Another cat ran alongside it and cuffed the other cat every time it hesitated. A trail of fire followed them before they disappeared, and as quickly as they had appeared and left, fresh flames flickered through the tiles.

Asta tingled all over. It was Ash and Beauty with Rathder in the same plague suit that had frightened her on her first day in the city. Ash was alive. She pressed against the willow box, searching the rooftop, but her brother had vanished.

Several boatmen and passengers sniggered. 'Calm down, woman,' a boatman abreast of the bejewelled woman scolded. 'It's just some nut in a plague suit fleeing the conflagration with his cats!'

'That was a demon *spreading* the fire,' she snapped back, but her comment only invited more people to guffaw.

Miriam squinted at the chimney breast. 'Was that Marcus Rathder and his cats?' she muttered under her breath. Cosima and Isaac looked across the rooftop. 'He was wearing his plague suit when I saw him in the street, watching his apothecary shop burn.'

At that moment, hot air gusted about boats, and the bejewelled woman wailed again. 'It's the breath of evil!'

Everyone on the water followed her gaze.

'The wind is changing direction.' Miriam stared at the smoke. It was no longer swirling westwards, but blowing from the north and furiously fanning the flames east. The blood drained from her face. 'It's heading for the Tower of London. The biggest supply of gunpowder in the country is stored there. If the Tower blows up, it will be catastrophic.'

The boatmen shared uneasy glances with their passengers and picked up their oars.

'My dream, the comet, the prophecy – it all makes sense,' Miriam said after a pause and a shake of her head before dashing to her baskets. She upturned them and tipped the contents into the boat. She snatched a roll of parchment, a bottle of ink and a quill and scribbled rapidly.

'Jet,' she said breathlessly, hurrying to him and cupping his head in her hands. 'Dearest, if you can understand me, then there is hope yet. Go to Whitehall and deliver this message to the queen. She must convince the king to create bigger fire breaks. Pulling down some houses isn't enough. If the king's men blow up whole streets and take the fuel away from the fire, it will save the city. The gunpowder will save the gunpowder.'

Jet listened, his eyes glinting intelligently.

'Go to your brothers, sisters and cousins at the Tower,'

Miriam went on. 'Work together. Find the queen as fast as you can then follow the king's soldiers into the fire. Use your voices. You can tell them exactly where the flames are heading and help them stop the blaze. Now go! Go!'

'Gunpowder!' Jet squawked. 'Firebreak!' and with a throaty croak, he launched into the sky.

Asta watched the raven's black wings pound through the air and disappear against the dark smoke swallowing the blue above. Her green eyes searched the rooftops again. As she looked, her heart summoned memories of Ash, of them play fighting in the forest and their mother joining in, softly cuffing them with her paws, of them failing to catch every fish, bird and rabbit they stalked, and of the three of them curled up at the end of each day in their den. But as Asta's gaze flittered across the city, her thoughts twisted. She saw them sprint through the bracken from the hunters, and the stout and thin man take their mother away. She felt the cold metal trap press against her fur, and she remembered the horror etched on Ash's face when they arrived at Rathder's Apothecary Shop. Then Beauty's copper eyes emerged, and Asta's fur prickled, hearing her silky tones and her caterwaul when she lay in her own blood on the floor. Asta's chest tightened, seeing Ash's gentle face darken with scorn. She remembered him watching Moore taking her away to the

Bartholomew Fair, and a hot, trembling fury thrummed through her as her mind flashed with animals chained to the baiting ring. She was going to take her brother away from the cruel greed and ambitions of humans, even if it was the last thing she ever did.

Asta looked at Lipa and remembered Tilia's mahogany eyes, glistening behind the bars of her cage the night before she rampaged through the fair and sacrificed herself for Asta's and Lipa's return to the wild.

Asta turned to the bear cub with guilt slicing through her. 'Lipa,' she said, and the bear cub gazed at her fondly, 'I can't leave London without Ash.' She shook her head. Lipa's face fell. 'This is my last chance to help him. I will never forgive myself for not trying one last time to take him with us. I have to find him.'

Lipa blinked for a moment, then pressed his head against hers. 'Go to your family, Asta.'

Asta nuzzled into his fur and breathed in his scent. 'Ash and I are your family too now.' She wanted to remember his sweetness and innocence forever. 'I'll be back soon,' she promised, her voice wavering, not knowing if she could honour it. 'Stay close to Miriam and the others. If anything happens to me, I know Miriam will make sure you reach the wild.' And with a lump of fear swelling her chest, she pawed the doors of the willow box open.

Asta burst free and hopped from one boat to the next as if they were stepping stones. Cosima, Isaac, Rosie and Miriam watched her, open-mouthed, startle every boatman and passenger in her path and then leap on to the wooden walkway, laid out on the dried, cracked mud. She bounded towards the city.

'What do we do?' Isaac gasped, leaping to the willow box and shutting Lipa away from any prying eyes. 'We'll never get her back!'

'It's all right,' Miriam said, a soft, impressed smile drawing across her lips as Asta reached the stone river wall and pulled herself on to the bank. 'She's gone to fetch her brother.'

CHAPTER TWENTY-SEVEN

INTO THE FIRE

Asta clambered up on to the stone bank and cantered forward with her heart pounding and her paws warming underfoot. Her eyes rushed over the ash-flecked rooftops, and she spotted the medieval church's squat bell tower close to where she had seen Rathder, Beauty and Ash. A fiery gale blustered about her fur, and her hind leg throbbed as she jumped into an uneven sprint with her eyes flicking across the crush of people trudging east. Her ears flattened, hearing the fire thrash through the city like waves crashing in a storm.

She weaved through the throngs of people and hurried into the dark labyrinth of narrow alleyways where the jettied houses grazed roofs overhead and obscured the sky and air above. Her breath was dense in her lungs as she veered down a lane. She searched for the medieval church and rounded into the lane to the left then to the right. She took turning after turning and desperation swept through her as each road she raced through had no church to be found. Panic was flooding her when she finally glimpsed it. She sprinted towards the squat tower and bounded through its churchyard's stone arch, crowned with three skulls.

The church's heavy timber doors were ajar. Asta slunk inside and galloped into the nave. She took in the stained-glass windows and upturned altar that had been looted of its brass crosses and chalices. She hurried to a spiral staircase, tucked away in the corner of the building, swerving round abandoned chests, furniture and stacks of paper left there for safekeeping by people who had fled the flames.

Up and up, she climbed, hoping that the dark, dizzyingly steep stairs would lead out on to the roof, but the tower was a sealed column of rock. Despair was gnawing at her when a shaft of light brightened the gloom, and she raced on. A few steps later, she found a window, cracked open to the city below, and she peered out on to a blanket of tiled roofs and clambered outside.

A blast of hot air hit her as she landed on the church roof with a wince. She caught her breath. The city stretched further than she could fathom. Rathder could have taken any route, slipped into any of the countless windows or sought shelter behind any of the thousands of chimneys before her. She heard the anxious coos of pigeons above her and the roar of the fire grow louder. She looked up at the birds flapping around their nests, perched on the medieval church tower, and felt a tug in her chest. Their lives were in peril, yet they would not abandon their young.

The smoke stung her eyes as her gaze darted to the Tower of London, looming over the houses to her left. She squinted, scanning every rooftop she could see. Her eyes rounded. There, in line with the Tower, she spied a fresh dark swirl and the flicker of flames, and a black-cloaked figure swiftly stooping and shuffling between chimneys as Ash raced across the rooftops in chains that Rathder threw out and yanked back towards him. Beauty pursued Ash with her tail held high.

Asta's heart drummed. She hunched low and stalked forward, cresting the rise and fall of the pitched rooftops through the smoke, and hid behind chimneystacks as she went. She was close enough to scent Rathder's sweat when Beauty, her grey fur mottled with patches of soot, stared in Asta's direction. Instantly, Asta flattened herself. She held her breath and bared her claws, but as the seconds dragged past she heard only a whip of wood and frustrated cries coming from the other side. She breathed easier and inched her head up.

'Come here, you insufferable *gib*!' Rathder yelled, vigorously jerking the chain.

It was then that Asta saw him. Ash was crouched with his paws hooked round a roof tile. His body was rigid with fear, and his eyes were glazed and staring. A metal harness was wrapped across his thin body, and each time Rathder tugged it by the chain, it bit into his blackened fur. Attached to it by another shorter chain was a ring of pitch, just like the one she had seen Moore spit on in Rathder's garden. It smouldered, and young flames danced between cracks and gaps in the roof tiles behind him, above people's abandoned homes.

Rathder stomped over to Ash and whipped his cane through the air beside him, but Ash remained in the same place. 'Move, you infernal animal!'

Beauty dashed to Ash, her tail puffing with malice. 'Get up! I am not taking your place!' She swiped her claws across his face, yet still he would not move. The wind fanned the flames in her direction and she leaped away with a terrified yowl before whirling back to hiss contemptuously at Ash, 'You *coward*!'

She sank her teeth into his shoulder, and Ash uttered a cry so forlorn that it shattered Asta's being. Her love for Ash and her hatred of Beauty and Rathder entwined, summoning a ferocity in her that she could not control. A trembling blaze of fury swept over her, numbing the ache in her hind leg. Her mind cleared of all fright, and with a fearsome snarl she hurtled over the rooftop.

'Leave him alone!' She rocketed into Beauty and they tumbled across the rooftops through the haze of smoke.

'*You!*' Beauty growled, boring her claws into Asta's injured leg. Asta howled, and Beauty growled with triumph. With an almighty flip and roll, Asta wrestled herself away.

Beauty and Asta glowered at one another, their noses wrinkling and their hackles stiffening, but a moment later, a searing thwack shot up Asta's spine.

'Get away from my Beauty!' Rathder walloped Asta with his cane again and pinned her to the roof with his boot, the mask on his face staring down at her malevolently as she tried to wriggle free. 'Despicable fiend! I'll kill you for escaping the fair and ruining me! It's *your* fault that London is burning!'

Asta scrunched up her eyes against the lashings of his cane. 'Ash!' she yelped, looking over to him in the blur, but he only stared into space and shuddered, knowing the sting of Rathder's rage too well. 'Please, Ash! Help me!'

Beauty watched Asta squirm under Rathder's foot, and her eyes flashed with pleasure. She padded over to Ash and nuzzled into his neck. 'Watch your master beat the evil out of your sister!' she purred. 'He is saving your life again. She was here to murder you!'

'NO!' Asta cried. 'Ash, I'm here to rescue you!'

'Lies!' Beauty spat. 'Don't listen to her!'

Asta flinched as Rathder's cane struck her again. 'You have to believe me, Ash! I love you. I need you. I'd do anything for you!'

Ash looked at her, and both their eyes gleamed with despair.

'You can't trust her,' Beauty hissed. 'She doesn't love you or need you and nor did your mother. Only my master and myself love you for who you are.'

'Die, vile creature!' Rathder bellowed, lifting his cane high above his head.

'Ash!' Asta whispered. '*Please!*'

Ash's jaw hardened.

'Squash the wild beast,' Beauty hissed. 'Just like her brother!'

Ash's pupils dilated. He flew at Rathder and burrowed his claws into his plague suit and shredded its waxed canvas gown. Rathder shrieked and his back arched in alarm as Ash raked Rathder's clammy, glistening skin and sank his fangs into the flesh at the nape of his neck. Rathder stumbled backwards, swiping his cane from side to side, and Ash's chain rattled as Rathder tried to shake him loose.

Relief surged through Asta. The pain throbbing through her body a moment before transformed into a hot burst of adrenaline. She hurtled into Beauty, who was chasing Ash up Rathder's clothes, and knocked her away. They somersaulted across the rooftop under a sinister red mist in the sky above.

The four of them brawled fiercely, unaware that a group of the king's troops raced through the streets below, where a cart laden with barrels followed two grandly dressed men on horseback and ground to a halt outside abandoned homes. As the cart stopped, more soldiers, drenched in sweat, scrambled from inside it and groaned, heaving the heavy drums on to the ground. Kicking in the wooden front doors as they went, they urgently rolled the barrels into the houses. In less than a minute, all but one soldier rejoined the cart, which was already moving to the next building. He chased after them, jogging backwards and looking over his shoulder as he carefully poured black powder from a large pouch.

A tall, regal man with thin lips and a long light-brown curled wig cantered to him. 'Take cover!' he ordered. The soldier nodded obediently and hurriedly trailed the powder as he chased after the cart, now trotting round a corner.

'Ignite!' a voice bellowed.

A second later, a spark zipped across the black powder towards the abandoned houses.

The force of the blast lifted Asta, Beauty, Rathder and Ash into the air. They slammed back on to the roof in a cloud of smoke and dust, and the tiles beneath them began toppling into a vacuum of heat below. Asta bounded across the debris, rapidly vanishing under her paws, with the petrified yowls of Beauty and Rathder ringing in her ears as they slid into the void below.

'Ash!' Asta yelled as she leaped blindly through the smoke, 'Jump! JUMP!'

Just when she wasn't sure whether she was flying or falling, her claws caught the uppermost, vertical timbers of the neighbouring house. A tremendous crash sounded, shaking every fibre of her body, and the building she had just left folded in on itself in a belch of soot, wood, wattle and daub.

Asta hung there in the smoke, her limbs shaking with effort. She coughed, her throat burning, 'Ash?' Her green eyes hunted the murk filled with embers floating on the wind. 'Ash?'

But she heard only the roar of the approaching fire.

'ASH?'

The gale gusted, clearing the cloud of destruction, and revealed a long drop and a mountain of rubble where an entire line of houses had been demolished. Asta stared into the destruction below. She was dangling from the last house standing.

'Ash!' she whimpered, scrunching up her eyes in pain. The grief of losing Ash now was too much to bear.

The building beneath her claws creaked and quaked. It would topple soon too.

'Asta?' a voice called somewhere from above. 'Asta? ASTA!'

She looked up with a gasp. Ash's striated face stared down at her from the roof. He leaned over the side and grabbed the scruff of her neck in his jaws and helped her on to the roof.

'Oh, Ash!' She rushed to him, his harness and chain jangling as they collapsed with relief and exhaustion upon the tiles.

'I'm sorry for everything, Asta,' Ash mewed, burrowing his face into her fur.

'I'm sorry too,' Asta sniffed, pressing her head against his. She smelled the stifling scent of fire and burnt fur on him. But she didn't care. It had been so long since she had felt close to him. She wished their hug would never end.

Just then, a guttural moan sounded deep within the building, and Asta and Ash yelped as the rooftop lurched to the left.

'Hurry,' Asta said, panting. Her eyes travelled over Ash's harness. It was fixed with the same kind of steel pins that Miriam had pulled from Asta's collar. 'We need to get this thing off you and make our way back to the river and find my friends.' She placed her front paws on Ash's shoulders. She pinched the pins between her teeth and pulled. First the harness, then Ash's collar fell away and Ash skittered to the side as it clanged upon the roof. Asta paused, great happiness rising within her. 'We're going back to the wild, Ash!' She beamed. 'Come on!'

They scrambled across the rooftop, but no matter which way they turned, there was no roof to jump to, no window to climb through or no other building to scale.

'No!' Ash cried. 'There has to be a way!'

The building shuddered beneath their paws. The wildcats hunched low, their eyes shining with despair. There was no way out.

Asta swallowed and shuffled to Ash. 'It's all right,' she said, trying to make her voice strong, but it caught in her throat, 'because, whatever happens, we're free. We're finally free.'

Ash stared at her and his face crumpled as he let out an exhausted sigh. He nodded softly. 'We're free.'

They curled up together as they used to beside their

mother in their den. Fear swept through them, but as the house beneath them began to splinter and snap, and the roar of the Great Fire sounded in their ears, they drew each other close.

Asta glanced up for one last glimpse of the sky. It was

then that she spied the flock of ravens soaring through the smoke, billowing across the blue. She thought of Jet and everything he had done for her and Lipa, and she breathed easier, knowing Jet and Miriam would do everything to keep the bear cub safe.

A deafening rumble shook them from below, and a spectacular crash made Ash lift his head from Asta's shoulder. 'Asta!' he gasped. 'Look!'

Asta followed his gaze, her eyes fluttering with disbelief. The majority of the house beneath them had collapsed, leaving a wreck of gnarled timber and plaster leading down to the ground far below.

Asta turned to Ash, their faces bright with hope.

The wildcats clambered down the debris to the street below, and as they bounded through the smoke, they disappeared from the human world, smouldering into ash behind them.

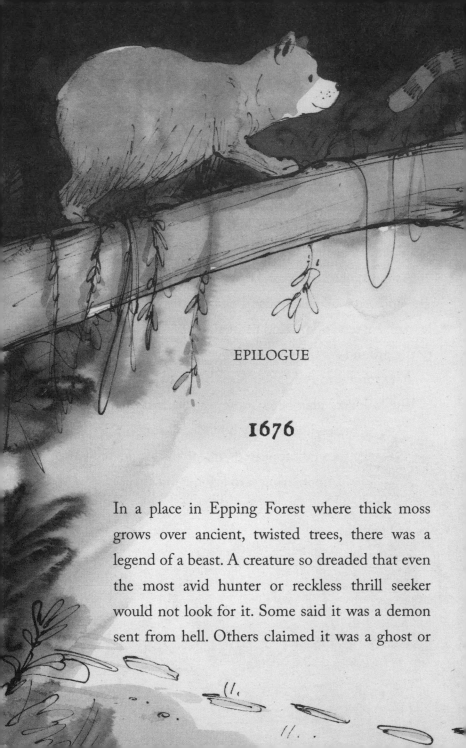

EPILOGUE

1676

In a place in Epping Forest where thick moss grows over ancient, twisted trees, there was a legend of a beast. A creature so dreaded that even the most avid hunter or reckless thrill seeker would not look for it. Some said it was a demon sent from hell. Others claimed it was a ghost or

a wild man. Those who saw it talked of
ghoulish, gleaming eyes, of dark fur, of
giant paws . . . a deep growl, a sinister hiss.

Only one person did not fear it. The person
who started the rumour ten years before. An old
woman with long white hair tied in a bun. She
would sometimes roam there, wearing a red cloak,
after each new moon.

'Smell this sweet valerian root,' she said, picking a tall,
flowery stem and inhaling deeply. She held it up to the raven
perching on her shoulder and its shaggy throat feathers
puffed with pleasure. 'It will bring peace to the worriers and

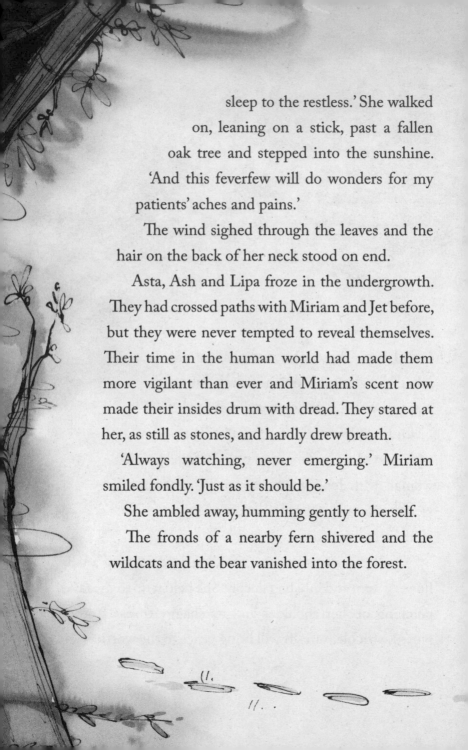

sleep to the restless.' She walked on, leaning on a stick, past a fallen oak tree and stepped into the sunshine. 'And this feverfew will do wonders for my patients' aches and pains.'

The wind sighed through the leaves and the hair on the back of her neck stood on end.

Asta, Ash and Lipa froze in the undergrowth. They had crossed paths with Miriam and Jet before, but they were never tempted to reveal themselves. Their time in the human world had made them more vigilant than ever and Miriam's scent now made their insides drum with dread. They stared at her, as still as stones, and hardly drew breath.

'Always watching, never emerging.' Miriam smiled fondly. 'Just as it should be.'

She ambled away, humming gently to herself.

The fronds of a nearby fern shivered and the wildcats and the bear vanished into the forest.

AUTHOR'S NOTE

Asta and Ash's story first came to me at the end of 2019 when *The State of Nature* report released data on nearly 700 species of land, freshwater and sea animals, fish, birds and butterflies. More than 41 per cent of UK native species studied had declined and 15 per cent of wildlife species were under threat from extinction. Some 133 species had already vanished from Britain since 1500.

Wildcats are Britain's rarest mammal. They are now found only in Scotland. On the brink of extinction, only thirty native cats remain. According to Roger Lovegrove's *Silent Fields: The Long Decline of a Nation's Wildlife*, the threat of extinction, along with other native species such as hedgehogs, badgers, pine martens and kites, stems from Henry VIII's and Elizabeth I's Vermin Acts. Bounties were paid for culling animals believed to pose a risk to livestock and grain. In the 17th century, almost 5,000 rewards for wildcat heads were claimed. And so began Asta and Ash's 17th century adventure.

For me, the Great Fire of London is the most memorable event of the 1600s. It's one of the most iconic moments in British history, yet there are not many children's books set during that time. The catastrophe started at the end of a very hot and dry summer in the early hours of 2 September 1666, not on Pudding Lane as most of us have been taught, but on today's Monument Street. Strong winds fanned the inferno and the smoke could be seen from Oxford. The burning lasted months, not days: Samuel Pepys's diary notes that cellars were still smouldering in March 1667. 13,000 houses and eighty-seven churches were lost, but only six deaths were recorded; a figure which is widely believed to be inaccurate. King Charles II and his brother the Duke of York fought the blaze and they really did use gunpowder to create large firebreaks to stop the stores of gunpowder in the Tower of London from exploding. Ultimately, modern London, most famously St. Paul's Cathedral, rose from the ashes.

Two comets appeared in 1664 and 1665, and were interpreted as harbingers of the Great Plague and the Great Fire respectively. People were also nervous that the biblical number 666 in 1666 indicated evil was brewing. Samuel Pepys wrote: 'For the whole year, the population of London had a great sense of foreboding, because the year had the number of the devil in it – 666.'

As early as the 15ᵗʰ century, Nostradamus and Mother Shipton both recorded visions predicting the Great Fire. In 1651, an astrologer named William Lilly printed a prophecy entitled *Monarchy or No Monarchy* that contained cryptic illustrations of the future of England, including a city being devoured by flames. Lilly was suspected of plotting the Great Fire. Rathder's vision was inspired by Lilly's.

To this day, there is a superstition that six ravens must be kept at the Tower of London to prevent the fall of the kingdom and country. It is commonly thought to have originated with Charles II, but some historians, including the Tower's official historian, believe the superstition to have been invented by the Victorians.

Miriam is inspired by the 17ᵗʰ century rebel physician, herbalist and astrologer Nicolas Culpeper who brought free healthcare to the masses and sought to treat every person no matter how poor they were. His influence has rippled throughout social health schemes and provided inspiration to the founders of the NHS.

It is true that the majority of doctors fled the city during the Great Plague and 40,000 cats and 200,000 dogs were killed to stop the spread. Many apothecaries, like Rathder, donned plague suits and 'helped' the afflicted. Not all of them were qualified and some stole from the dead. Rathder's 17th century apothecary's shop is based on a photograph from the Wellcome Historical Medical Museum and library archives.

There was a real plot to burn London, which was due to take place on 3 September 1666. Rathder's name is an amalgamation of the surnames of the men who were convicted of the crime in April 1666, John Rathbone and William Saunders. He also lives in Gunpowder Alley, which is the same place where a corrupt apothecary lived and is documented in the Great Fire exhibition at the Museum of London. He also poisoned his customers.

A bear called Blind Bess was shot by the Puritans at the Hope Theatre on 9 February 1656. Baiting was a popular sport in Britain from the 12th until the 19th century, and the Bartholomew Fair opened every year between 1133 until 1855. Tragically, I don't think any bears escaped their fate.

Mysterious bear sightings were recorded in the Hackney Marshes in 1981, Epping Forest in 2008 and in the Lea Valley in East London in 2012, although brown bears have been extinct in Britain for more than 1,000 years.

No wildcats have roamed England and Wales for at least 150 years. Hopefully there is still time to save them.

ACKNOWLEDGEMENTS

Fire Cats has had its challenges: the pandemic, my first pregnancy (six and a half months of which I spent alone), the steep yet joyful learning curve of being a new mum, then the sudden death of a friend, dear Timothy John Robert Nesbitt QC, who is terribly missed. Writing this book has been a fortunate and happy distraction from the madness of the world and I am beyond glad that it is finally out. There are some people I must thank who have helped me along the way.

To my friends and family who kept me sane, particularly Alex Leggett, Charis Edwards, Tom Aldridge, Guljeet Sahney, Zoe Blanc, Letty Peto, Kate Stone, Daisy Fernandes, Tascha Weatherby, Camille Akass, Harriet Pounds, Ashleigh Hanson, Nihara Krause, Alfie and Kim Biddle, Oli Swan; my brothers, Matthew Fargher and Ed Fargher; my parents Tim and Lizzie Fargher.

To my wonderful agent and friend, Chloe Seager, and to the rest of the team at Madeleine Milburn.

To my kind, patient and talented editor Sarah Hughes,

my copy-editor, Sam Stanton Stewart, proofreader, Natalie Young; to Amy Boxshall and everyone at Macmillan Children's Books. You are a joy to work with.

To my illustrator, Sam Usher, who has outdone himself once again and who had to work by candlelight during a storm to get the final illustrations for this book done.

To the Museum of London for their brilliant Great Fire exhibition. Go.

To the writers who informed the historical context: Ian Mortimer for *A Time Traveller's Guide to Restoration Britain;* to Neil Hanson for *The Dreadful Judgement: The True Story of the Great Fire of London*; to Rebecca Rideal for *1666: Plague, War and Hellfire*. Channel 5's documentary, *The Great Fire,* also helped me and Miriam paraphrases Professor Ronald Hutton's note in the series that the 'gunpowder saved the gunpowder'.

And to you, dear reader. Thank you for joining me on Asta and Ash's journey. I really hope you have enjoyed it.

ABOUT THE AUTHOR

Anna Fargher was raised in a creative hub on the Suffolk coast by an artist and a ballet teacher. She read English Literature at Goldsmiths before working in the British art world and opening her own gallery. *The Umbrella Mouse* was her first book, which she wrote on her phone's notepad during her daily commute on the London Underground. It was the winner of the Sainsbury's Children's Book Prize for Fiction and selected as Children's Book of the Month in Waterstones.

Anna lives in London and Suffolk.

ABOUT THE ILLUSTRATOR

Sam Usher graduated from the University of West England and his debut picture book *Can You See Sassoon?* was shortlisted for the Waterstones Prize and the Red House Children's Book Award. He is particularly admired for his technical drawing skill and prowess with watercolour. Also a talented pianist, when he's not holding a pen and wobbling it at paper, you'll find him perfecting a fiendishly difficult piece of Chopin.